Please return or renew by
latest date below

LOANS MAY BE RENEWED BY PHONE

W9-AFG-564

BEASTS

❋ *BEASTS* ❋

JOHN CROWLEY

DOUBLEDAY & COMPANY, INC.

GARDEN CITY, NEW YORK 1976

All of the characters in the book
are fictitious, and any resemblance
to actual persons, living or dead,
is purely coincidental.

Library of Congress Cataloging in Publication Data

Crowley, John.
Beasts.

I. Title.
PZ4.C9533Be   [PS3553.R597]   813'.5'4
ISBN 0-385-11260-2
Library of Congress Catalog Card Number 75–40719

For my mother

If thou wert the lion, the fox would
beguile thee; if thou wert the lamb,
the fox would eat thee; if thou wert
the fox, the lion would suspect thee,
when peradventure thou wert accused by
the ass: if thou wert the ass, thy
dullness would torment thee, and still
thou livedst but as a breakfast to the
wolf . . . What beast couldst thou be,
that were not subject to a beast?

—*Timon of Athens,* IV, iii

ONE

The shot tower

Loren Casaubon thought of himself as a lover of solitude. He hadn't chosen fieldwork in ethology strictly for that reason, but he thought of it as an asset in his work that he could bear—and believed he preferred—the company of the wild and the inhuman. The old shot tower and its new ferocious inhabitants, which Loren was to spend a summer nurturing, suited him exactly. He had laughed aloud when he first saw it, responding immediately to its lonely intransigence: he felt he had come home.

Because it lay hidden in the last few folds of wooded hills before the low country began, the shot tower, despite its hundred-foot height, came into view without warning. It seemed to step suddenly out of the mountain granite and across the road to block the way; or to have stood up suddenly from sleep on hearing the approach of a man. For over two centuries it had had no human company. The vast lowlands pocked with marshes that slid from the mountains' margins down to the sea, which the tower guarded as though it were the utmost watchtower of a mountain warlord, were inhabited only by wild things.

Whatever foresightless pioneer it was who had planned this marsh-aborted industrial development here so long ago had gotten no further than the tower and a few stone outbuildings. All that had been made of wood was gone now. The canal that he had counted on to bring him into touch with the rest of the manufacturing world had ended in bankruptcy forty miles away. He must have been more dreamer than businessman anyway, Loren decided when he first encountered the tower. It should have been a purely utilitarian structure, a factory for the making of lead bullets; its striking slim height was necessary only so that molten lead, poured through sieves at the top, had time as it fell to form into perfect round balls like leaden raindrops before striking an annealing tank of water at the bottom. But the builder had been unable to resist the obvious romantic associations his tall, round, granite tower had, and in fact had made a castle keep, grimly Gothic, with narrow, ogive arrow slits and a castellated top. It was a fake feudal keep in a new world, whose only true affinity with real castles was its reason for being: war.

That reason had long passed. The ingenuity of the tower and its lead shot had been long supplanted by more horrid ingenuities. It had had, until Loren came, no function but its absurd picturesqueness. Loren brought it a new purpose: it was to be a substitute cliff for four members of a nearly extinct race of cliff-dwellers.

He could feel motion inside the cardboard box when he lifted it from the carrier of his bike. He put the box on the ground and opened it. Inside, the four white birds, quilly and furious, set up a raucous squawking. Alive and well. Biking them in had been harrowing, but there was no other way to get into the area; the rutted road had brought his heart to his mouth at every carefully negotiated bump. He laughed at himself now for his scruples. Healthy and strong as young devils, the four immature peregrine falcons, two males and two females, looked harmful and unharmable. Their fiercely drawn brows and hooked beaks belied their infancy; their crying was angry and not pitiful. They, of course, couldn't know that they were among the last of their kind.

The process of breeding peregrine falcons in captivity and then returning them to the wild—a kind of reverse falconry, which in fact used many ancient falconers' techniques—had begun years ago in that rush of sentiment about wildlife and wild places that had rendered the word "ecology" useless. Like all rushes of sentiment, it was short-lived. The falcon-breeding program had been curtailed along with a thousand other, more ambitious programs—but it had not quite died. The handling of feral birds was a skill so demanding, a challenge so compelling, that like the old falconry it had proved self-perpetuating. The small band of correspondents engaged in it were a brotherhood; their craft was as difficult, esoteric, and absorbing as that of Zen monks or masters of Go. Their efforts were, almost certainly, all that kept peregrines in existence; just as certainly, if they stopped, extinction would follow. The falconers were too few; and the birds they released were too few to find each other easily to mate once they were free. Some studies Loren had read put the survival rate for large aerial predators released from captivity at twenty per cent. Of these, perhaps a tenth mated and raised young. So, without Loren and the others, all sponsored by quixotic foundations or unguarded university departments, the falcon would disappear from this continent. The proudest and most independent of winged things had become, in an odd sense, parasitic to man.

Holding the box carefully level, Loren ducked through the arched door and into the tower. Inside, not even the spooky, narrow bars of dust-filled sunlight from the arrow slits could disguise the fact that this place had after all been a factory. The narrow spiral staircase that went up to the top was iron; it rang dully beneath Loren's boots. At various levels the iron struts of platforms remained; from each level a different size of shot would have been dropped: dust shot from forty feet, bird shot from higher, buck shot still higher; musket balls from the topmost platform, which was still intact, though a large section of castellated wall had fallen away and the platform was only half roofed. It was here that Loren had built his nesting box, a barred cage for the birds' first weeks. He had placed it facing the gap in the wall so that the birds, even while caged, could look out over their domain.

The wind was strong at this height; it tossed Loren's thick, dark hair and tickled his beard. Without haste he opened the nesting box and one by one placed his four round feather-dusters inside. He could feel their quick heartbeats, and their young talons griped his hands strongly. Once inside, they ceased to cry out; they roused and shook down their disturbed plumage in miniature imitation of the way they would rouse when they were fully grown.

From his many-pocketed coat Loren took out the paper-wrapped bits of steak and the forceps. With the forceps he would feed them, and with the same forceps remove their droppings—"mutes" to the falconer—just as their parents' beaks would have done. They gulped the raw meat hungrily, beaks wide; they ate till their crops were stuffed.

When he had finished, he locked the box and climbed to the gap. He stood there squinting into the wind, looking with his weak human eyes over the thousand acres of tree line, field, marsh, and sea coast that would be his falcons' hunting ground. He thought he could see, far off, a faint white glare where the sea began. There were probably three hundred species of bird and animal out there for his birds to hunt: rabbits, larks, blackbirds, frogs, starlings, and even ducks for the larger and swifter females to catch. "Duck hawk" was the old American name for the peregrine, given it by the farmers who shot it on sight as a marauder, just as they called the red-tailed hawk a chicken hawk. A narrow perspective; certainly neither the peregrine nor the nearly extinct red-tail had ever lived exclusively or even largely on domestic fowl; but Loren understood the farmer. Every species interprets the world in its own terms only. Even Loren, who served the hawks, knew that his reasons were a man's reasons and not a bird's. He looked around him once more, made certain that his charges lacked nothing, that their basin was full (they rarely drank, but soon they would begin to bathe), and then went clanking back down the iron stairway, pleased at the thought that he was settled in now, with a task to do, and alone.

Before bringing in the birds he had established himself at the tower. He had biked in supplies for a three-month stay: medicine, a bedroll, a heater and a stove, food, two shotguns and ammunition. The greater part of his duties over the next month or so would be to hunt for his falcons until they could do so for themselves. Unless they became familiar with the sight and taste of feral prey, they might be unable to recognize it as food—they might kill birds, because powerful instincts commanded it, but they might not know enough to eat what they killed. Loren must every day produce fresh-killed game for them to eat.

It was too late in the day now to go out, though; he would start the next morning. He had toyed with the idea of bringing in an adult trained hawk and hunting with it for his young ones; but—even though the immense difficulties of this plan intrigued him—in the end he decided against it; if for any of a thousand reasons the adult couldn't catch enough to feed the young, it would be his fault. The life his hawks must be prepared for was so arduous that they must have all his attention now.

He sat a long time outside the door of the stone building he had outfitted for himself, while the endless twilight lingered, fading from dusty yellow to lucent blue. Far above him in their tower his hawks would be grooming, tucking down their fierce heads, growing still, and at last sleeping. Loren had not enough duties to occupy his nights, and though he would go to sleep early, to be up before dawn, still he felt some anxiety over the blank hours of darkness ahead: anxiety that was causeless and that he never allowed to rise quite into consciousness. He made a simple meal meticulously and ate it slowly. He ordered his stores. He prepared for the next morning's hunt. He lit a lamp and began to look through the magazines.

Whoever it was that had camped here—last summer, he judged by the magazines' dates—had been an omnivorous reader, or looker anyway; they were mostly picture magazines. The camper had left few other traces of himself—some broken wine bottles and empty cans. From some impulse to purify his quarters for his own monkish purposes, Loren at first had thought to burn these magazines. They seemed intrusive on his solitude, freighted as they were with human wishes and needs and boredoms. He hadn't burned them. Now almost guiltily he began to leaf through them.

North Star was a government magazine he had not often bothered to look at. This issue was a fat one, "Celebrating a Decade of Peace and Autonomy." On its cover was the proud blond head of the Director of the Northern Autonomy, Dr. Jarrell Gregorius. Doctor of what? Loren wondered. An honorific, he supposed; just as it was an honorific to call the last ten years peaceful simply because they had not been years of total war.

Ten years ago the partition of the American continent had ended years of civil war. Almost arbitrarily—as quarreling parents and children retreat into separate rooms and slam doors on one another—ten large Autonomies and several smaller ones—independent city-states, mostly—had formed themselves out of the senescent American nation. They quarreled endlessly among themselves, and also with the stub of Federal government that still remained, supposedly as an arbitrator but in fact as an armed conspiracy of old bureaucrats and young technocrats desperately trying to retain and advance their power, like a belligerent old Holy Roman Empire intent on controlling rebellious princedoms. For young people of Loren's persuasion the long and still-continuing struggle had given rise to one great good: it had halted, almost completely, the uniform and mindless "development" of the twentieth century; halted the whole vast machine of Progress, fragmenting it, even (which had never in the old days seemed possible) forced its wheels to grind in reverse. All the enormous and prolonged sufferings that this reversal had brought on a highly civilized nation long dependent on resource management, on development, on the world of artifacts, could not alter Loren's pleasure in watching or reading about the old wilderness reclaiming a recreational facility or the grass covering silently the scars of strip mines and military bases.

So he looked kindly on the vain doctor. If it was only vanity and stupidity that had precipitated the partition, and kept these impotent little pseudonations alive and at one another's throats, then a theory of Loren's—not his alone—was proved out: that even the flaws of a certain species can contribute to the strength of the earth's whole life.

It may be now, though—the magazine gave some hints of it—that people had "learned their lesson" and felt it was time to consider plans for reunification. This same Dr. Gregorius thought so. Loren doubted whether the blood and the hatreds could be so quickly forgotten. "Independence," political independence, was a vast, even a silly myth; but it was less harmful than the myths of unity and interdependence that had led to the old wars: less harmful anyway to that wild world that Loren loved better than the lives and places of men. Let men be thrown onto their own resources, let them re-create their lives in small; let them live in chaos, and thus lose their concerted power to do harm to the world: that's what independence meant, practically speaking, whatever odd dreams it was dressed in in men's minds. Loren hoped it would last. Our great, independent Northern Autonomy. Long may it wave. He let the pages of *North Star* flutter together and was about to throw it back on the pile when a photograph caught his eye.

This might have been Gregorius as a boy. It was in fact his son, and there were differences. The father's face seemed to possess a fragile, commanding strength; the son's face, less chiseled, the eyes darker-lashed and deeper, the mouth fuller, seemed more willful and dangerous. It was a compelling, not a commanding, face. A young, impatient godling. His name was Sten. Loren folded the magazine open there and propped it beneath the lamp. When he had undressed and done his exercises, the boy watching, he turned down the lamp; the boy faded into darkness. When he awoke at dawn, the face was still there, pale in the gray light, as though he too had just awakened.

There is a certain small madness inherent in solitude; Loren knew that. He would soon begin to talk aloud, not only to the birds but to himself as well. Certain paths in his consciousness would become well-trodden ways because there was no other impinging consciousness to deflect him. A hundred years ago, Yerkes—one of the saints in Loren's brief canon—had said about chimpanzees that one chimpanzee is no chimpanzee. Men were like that too, except that eidetic memory and the oddity of self-consciousness could create one or a dozen others for a man alone to consort with: soon Loren would be living alone in company, the company of selves whom he could laugh with, chastise, chat with; who could tyrannize him, entertain him, bedevil him.

At noon he split with his sheath knife the skulls of the three quail he had shot and offered the brains to his charges: the best part. "Now look, there are only three among the four of you—none of that now—what's the matter? Eat, damn you—here, I'll break it up. God, what manners . . ." He let them tear at one of the quail while he dressed the other two for later. He watched the falcons' tentative, miniature voracity with fascination. He looked up; heavy clouds were gathering from the sea.

The next day it rained steadily, somberly, without pause. He had to light his lamp to go on with his magazines; he wore a hat against the dripping from the rotted ceiling. A chipmunk took refuge with him in the house, and he thought of trying to catch it for his hawks, but let it stay instead. Twice he splashed over to the tower and fed the birds steak and the remnants of quail, and returned through the puddles to his place by the lamp.

There was a fascination in the year-old news magazines, so breathlessly reporting transience, giving warnings and prophecies, blithely assuming that the biases and fashions of the moment were the heralds of new ages, would last forever. He speculated, turning the damp pages, on what a man of, say, a century ago would make of these cryptic, allusive stories. They would be—style aside—much like the stories of his own time in their portentous short sight. But they reflected a world utterly changed.

USE calls for quarantine of free-living leos. No search of this paper would reveal that USE stood for the Union for Social Engineering. What would his reader make of that acronym?

And what on earth would he make of the leos?

"It was a known fact—about mice and men, for instance—but the real beginning was with tobacco," the article began. Figure that out, Loren said to the reader he had invented. Opaque? Mysterious? In fact a cliché; every article about the leos told this tale. "They had long known, that is, that the protective walls of cells could be broken down, digested with enzymes, and that the genetic material contained in the cells could fuse to form hybrid cells, having the genetic characteristics of both—of mice and of men, say. This they could do; but they could not make them grow." Sloppy science, Loren thought, even for a popular magazine. He explained aloud about cell fusion to his nonplussed reader, then continued with the article: "Then in 1972"—just about the time Loren imagined this being read—"two scientists fused the cells of two kinds of wild tobacco—a short, shaggy-leafed kind, and a tall, sparse kind—and *made it grow:* a medium-tall, medium-shaggy plant which, furthermore, would reproduce its own kind exactly, without further interference. A new science—*diagenetics*—was born." Sciences are made, not born, Loren put in; and no science has ever been called diagenetics, except by the press. "In the century since, this science has had two important results. One is food: gigantic, high-protein wheat, tough as weeds." And as tasteless, Loren added. "Plants that grow edible fruits above ground, edible tubers below. Walnuts the size of grapefruits, with soft shells." And if anyone had listened to them, been capable, in those years, of Reason, had not preferred the pleasures of civil war, partition, and religious zeal, the lowlands that Loren's tower commanded might now be covered with Walnato orchards, or fields of patent Whead.

"The other result was, of course, the leos," the article went on placidly. And without further explanation, having performed its paper-of-record duties, it went on to explicate the intricacies of the USE proposals for a quarantine. It was left up to Loren, in the rest of that wet, confining day, to try to make sense out of the leos for the reader he had summoned up and could not now seem to dismiss.

There had been cell-fusion experiments with animals, with vertebrates, with mammals finally. The literature was full of their failures. No matter how sophisticated the engineering, the statistical possibility of failure in cell fusion, given all the possible genetic combinations, was virtually limitless; it wouldn't have been surprising if only dead ends had resulted forever. But life *is* surprising; *your* era's belief that one sort of life is basically hostile to another has long been disproven, is in fact if you think about it self-evidently false. We are, each of us living things, nothing but a consortium of other living things in a kind of continual parliamentary debate, dependent on each other, living on each other, no matter how ignorant we are of it; penetrating each others' lives "like—like those hawks in the tower are dependent on me, and I am too on them, though we don't need to know it to get on with it. . . ."

So it happened that with skill and a growing body of theoretical knowledge, scientists (in a playful mood, Loren explained, having saved the world from hunger) created more grotesques than any old-time sideshow had ever pretended to exhibit. Most of them died hours after leaving their artificial wombs, unable to function as the one or as the other; or they survived in a limited sense, but had to be helped through brief and sterile lives.

The cells of the lion and the man, though, joined like a handshake, grew, and flourished. And bore live young like themselves. There was no way of explaining why this union should be so successful; the odds against a lion and a butterfly combining successfully were almost as high.

It was the Sun, the leos have come to believe, the Sun their father that brought them forth strong, and said to them: increase and multiply.

Loren stopped pacing out his small house. He realized that for some time he had been lecturing aloud, waving his arms and tapping his right forefinger against his left palm to make points. Faintly embarrassed, he pulled on his tall Irish rubber boots and stomped out into the wet to clear his head. It was unlikely that in this weather any rabbits would have visited his amateur (and very illegal) wire snares, but he dutifully checked them all. By the time he returned, the evening sky, as though with a sigh of relief, had begun to unburden itself of cloud.

Much later, moving with difficulty in the confines of his bag, he watched the horned moon climb up the sky amid fleeing cloudlets. He hadn't slept, still strung up from a day indoors. He had been explaining about the Union for Social Engineering to a certain John Doe dressed in a brown twentieth-century suit, with eyeglasses on. He understood that this person, invented by him only that day, had now moved in permanently to join his solitude.

"Welcome to the club," he said aloud.

* * *

It was raining softly again when Loren, at the end of the month, biked from the tower to the nearest town. He needed some supplies, and there might be mail for him at the post-office-store. The journey was also in the nature of a celebration: tomorrow, if it was fair, and it promised to be, he would open the nesting box for good. His falcons would fly: or at least be free to do so when the physical imperatives so precisely clocked up within them had come to term. From now on he would be chiefly observer, sometimes servant, physician possibly. They would be free. For a time they would return to the tower where they had been fed. But, unless they appeared to be ill or hurt, he wouldn't feed them. His job as parent was over. He would starve them till they hunted. That would be hard, but had to be; hunger would be the whip of freedom. And in two or three years, when they had reached sexual maturity, if they hadn't been shot, or strangled in electric wires, or poisoned, or suffered any of a thousand fates common to wild raptors, two of them might return to the tower, to their surrogate cliff, and raise a brood of quilly young. Loren hoped to be there to see.

His bike's tiny engine, which he shut off when the way was level and he could pedal, coughed as the tires cast up gauzy wings from the puddly road; Loren's poncho now and then ballooned and fluttered around him in the rainy breeze, as though he were rousing plumage preparatory to flight. He sang: his tuneless voice pleased no one but himself, but there was no one else to hear it. He stopped, as though hushed, when the rain-cut dirt road debouched onto the glistening blacktop that led to town.

He had a festive breakfast—his first fresh eggs in a month—and sipped noisily at the thick white mug of real coffee. The newspaper he had bought reported local doings, mostly, and what appeared to be propaganda generated by the Fed. This southernmost finger of the Northern Autonomy lay close to the coastal cities that, like the ancient Vatican States, huddled around the capital and enjoyed the Fed's protection. And the Fed's voice was louder than its legal reach. President calls for return to sanity. He laughed, and belched happily; he went out smoking a cheap cigar that burned his mouth pleasantly with a taste of town and humanity.

There was a single letter for him in his box at the store. It bore the discreet logo of the quasi-public foundation he worked for:

"Dear Mr. Casaubon: This will serve as formal notice that the

Foundation's Captive Propagation Program has been dissolved. Please disregard any previous instructions of or commitments by the Foundation. We are of course sorry if this change of program causes you any inconvenience. If you wish any instructions on return of stores, disposal of stock, etc., please feel free to write. Yours, D. Small, Program Supervisor."

It was as though he had been, without knowing it, in one of those closets in old-time fun houses that suddenly collapse floorless and wall-less and drop you down a wide, tumbling chute. Any inconvenience . . .

"Can I use your phone?" he asked the postmaster, who was arranging dry cereal.

"Sure. It's there. Um—it's not free."

"No. Of course. They'll pay at the other end."

The man wouldn't take this in; he continued to stare expectantly at Loren. With a sudden wave of displaced rage at the man, Loren chewed down on his cigar, glaring at him and fumbling furiously for money. He found a steel half-dollar and slapped it on the counter. The Foundation's money, he thought.

"Dr. Small, please."

"Dr. Small is in conference."

"This is Loren Casaubon. *Dr.* Loren Casaubon. I'm calling long distance. Ask again."

There was a long pause, filled with the ghost voices of a hundred other speakers and the ticking, buzzing vacuum of distance.

"Loren?"

"What the hell's going on? I just came to town today—"

"Loren, I'm sorry. It's not my decision."

"Well, whose idiot decision was it? You can't just stop something like this in the middle. It's criminal, it's . . ." He should have waited to call, taken time to marshal arguments. He felt suddenly at a loss, vulnerable, as though he might splutter and weep. "What *reason* . . ."

"We've been under a lot of pressure, Loren."

"Pressure. Pressure?"

"There's a big movement against this kind of wildlife program just now. We spend public money . . ."

"Are you talking about USE?"

There was a long pause. "They somehow got hold of our books. Loren, all this is very confidential." His voice had grown dim. "A lot of money was being wasted on what could be called, well, unimportant programs." He cleared his throat as though to forestall Loren's objections. "A scandal might have brewed up. *Would* have brewed up: frankly, they intended to make an example of us. The foundation couldn't afford that. We agreed to co-operate, you know, rationalize our programs, cut out the fat—"

"You bastard." There was no answer. "My birds will die."

"I put off sending the letter as long as I could. Isn't your first month's program complete? I tried, Loren."

His voice had grown so small that Loren's rage abated. He was angry with the wrong man. "Yes. The month is up. And if I spend another two months with them, it might—just *might* give them the edge to make it. No assurances."

"I'm sorry."

"I'm staying, Dr. Small. I never got this letter."

"Don't do that, Loren. It would embarrass me. This arrangement's very new. They're very—thorough, these USE people. It could harm you badly."

Till that moment, he hadn't thought of himself. Suddenly, his future unrolled before him like a blank blacktop road. There weren't many jobs around for solitary, queer, rageful ethologists with borderline degrees.

"Listen, Loren." Dr. Small began to speak rapidly, as though to overwhelm any objections; as though he were hurrying out a gift for a child he had just made cry. "I've had a request put to me to find a, well, a kind of tutor. A special kind. Someone like yourself, who can ride and hunt and all that, but with good academic qualifications. The choice is pretty much mine. Two children, a boy and a girl. A *special* boy and girl. Excellent benefits."

Loren said nothing. He understood of course that he was being bribed. He disliked the feeling, but some dark, fearful selfishness kept him from dismissing it angrily. He only waited.

"The trouble is, Loren, you'd have to take it up immediately."
Still no surrender. "I mean right away. This man isn't used to
having his requests lying around."

"Who is it?"

"Dr. Jarrell Gregorius. The children are his." This was meant
to be the coup, the master stroke; and for an odd reason that
Small couldn't know, it was.

With a sense that he was tearing out some living part of himself, a tongue, a piece of heart, Loren said tonelessly: "I'd have
to have certain conditions."

"You'll take it."

"All right."

"What?"

"I said all right!" Then, more conciliatory: "I said all right."

"As soon as you can, Loren." Small sounded deeply relieved.
Almost hearty. Loren hung up.

On the way back, tearing through thin rags of mist, Loren al-
ternated between deep rage and a kind of heart-sinking expectation.

USE! If the old Federal government were the Holy Roman
Empire, then the Union for Social Engineering was its Jesuits:
militant, dedicated, selfless, expert propagandists, righteous pro-
ponents of ends that justified their means. Loren argued fiercely
aloud with them, the crop-headed, ill-dressed, intent "spokes-
men" he had seen in the magazines; argued the more fiercely because they had beaten him, and easily. And why? For what?
What harm had his falcons done to their programs and plans?
Not desiring power himself, Loren couldn't conceive of someone
acting solely to gain it, by lying, compromise, indirection, by not
seeing reason. If a man could be shown the right of a case—and
surely Loren was right in this case—and then he didn't do it, he
appeared to Loren to be a fool, or mad, or criminal.

Reason, of course, was exactly what USE claimed it did see:
sanity, an end to fratricidal quibblings, a return to central planning and rational co-operation, intelligent use of the planet for
man's benefit. The world is ours, they said, and we must make it
work. Humbly, selflessly, they had set themselves the task of sav-
ing man's world from men. And it was frightening as much as

angering to Loren how well their counterreformation was getting on: USE had come to seem the last, best hope of a world helplessly bent on self-destruction.

Loren admitted—to himself, at least—that his secret, secretly growing new paradise was founded on man's self-destructive tendency, or at least that tendency in his dreams and institutions. He saw it as evolutionary control. USE saw it as a curable madness. So did many hungry, desperate, fearful citizens: more every day. USE was the sweet-tongued snake in this difficult new Garden, and the old Adam, whose long, sinful reign over a subservient creation had seemed to be almost over, expiated in blood and loss, was being tempted to lordship again.

＊

At evening he waited on top of the tower for the hawks to return. He had made up a box from the slatting of their outgrown nest boxes, and he carried a hood and wore a falconer's glove. He had brought the hood in with him in order to spend the long evenings embroidering and feathering it. Now he held it in his hand, not knowing whether it would mean betrayal or salvation for the hawk who would wear it.

They paid no attention to him when they arrived one by one at the tower. He was an object in their universe, neither hawk nor hawk's prey, and thus irrelevant: for they couldn't know he was the author of their lives. Hawks have no gods.

They hadn't eaten, apparently; none of their crops was distended. They took a long time to settle, hungry and restless; but as the sun bloodied the west, they began to rest. Loren chose the smaller of the two males. To bind his wings he used one of his socks, with the toe cut off. He seized him, and had slipped the sock over his body before the bird was fully aware. He shrieked once, and the others rose up, black shapes in the last light, free to fly. They settled again when they had expressed their indignation, and by that time their brother was bound and hooded. They took no notice.

In the room where he had expected to spend the summer, Loren collected his few personal belongings: the guns, the clothes, the notebooks. Let them worry about the supplies. If they wanted to make a cost accounting, they could do it without him.

The *North Star* magazine still stood propped under the lamp, open to the picture of Sten Gregorius. Beneath it on the floor was the box containing the tiercel peregrine falcon: tribute to the young prince. This one, anyway, would survive, taken care of, provided for. The three in the tower, free, might not survive. If they could choose, which life would they choose?

Which would he?

He put on his hat. There was still just enough light to start for town tonight. He didn't want to wake here in the morning, could not have borne seeing the hawks leave the tower at dawn under the press of hunger. Better to go now, and pedal his rage into exhaustion. Maybe then he could sleep.

He turned out the lamp and tossed the magazine into a corner with the others.

All right, he thought. I'll teach him. I'll teach him.

TWO

Sphinx

If a lion could talk, we would not understand him.
—Wittgenstein

He called himself Painter.

It was rare to see a leo come so far north; Caddie had never seen one. She knew them only from the pictures in her school-books: yellow sun, yellow land, the leo standing far off at a sod hut's door with one of his wives. The pictures were remote and unimpressive. But once she had dreamed of a leo. She had been sent to him on some business by her father. He lived in a place of stifling heat, which was lined with asbestos, as though to keep it from consuming itself. She panted, trying to draw breath, waiting with growing dread for the leo to appear. She felt the thunder of dream realization: she had come to the wrong house, she shouldn't be here, it wasn't the leo but the Sun who lived here: that was why it was so hot. She awoke as the leo appeared, suddenly, towering over her; he was simply a lion standing like a man, yet his face glowed as though made of molten gold, and his mane streamed whitely from his face. He seemed furious at her.

Painter was not a lion. He didn't tower over her; she kept her distance; yet he was massive enough. And he wasn't furious. He spent his time in his room, or at a table in the bar, and never spoke, except rarely to Hutt. She saw him take a telephone call, long distance; he said "Yes," holding the receiver slightly away from his head, and then only listened, and hung up without a farewell.

Tonight he sat at a table where she could see him from the laundry door. The bar was lit with smoky lanterns, and the smoke of the black cigarettes he smoked one after another rose into the lantern's light and hung like low clouds.

"I wonder where his wife is," she said to Hutt when he came to the door of the laundry. "Don't they always have a wife with them, wherever they go?"

"I'd just as soon not ask," Hutt said. "And neither had you better."

"Does he stink?"

"No more than me." Hutt grinned a gap-tooth grin at her and tossed her an armload of gray sheets.

Hutt was afraid of Painter, that was evident, and it was easy to see why. The leo's wrists were as square and solid as beams, and the muscles of his arm glided and slid like oiled machinery when he merely put out a cigarette. Hutt got so few customers that he usually toadied up to any new face; but not this face. The leo seemed quite satisfied with that.

Later that evening, though, on her way out to the goat shed to lock up, she saw Hutt and the leo conferring in the deserted bar. Hutt was counting something off on his fingers. When she passed, both of them looked up at her. The eyes of the leo were as golden as lamps, as large as lamps, and as unwavering. What had he to do with her? When she looked questioningly at Hutt, he avoided her look.

Caddie's parents had been professionals—industrial relations, whatever that meant; when she was a kid she often recited it to herself, as an exiled princess might recite her lineage. They hadn't fared well as refugees when the civil wars started down south. Her father had cut his foot, stupidly, while chopping wood, developed an infection, and just quietly died from it, as though that were the best he could manage under the circumstances. Her mother wasn't long in following. When she stopped telling Caddie about the wealth and comfort and respect they all had had, back before Caddie could clearly remember, she began to resign from life as well. Once a month the doctor from town would come out and look at her and go away. She caught a cold when it snowed in May, and died from it.

That left Caddie, fourteen, with two choices: the whorehouse at Bend, or indenture. She had almost decided on the whorehouse, was almost in a fearful way looking forward to it, like a girl setting out for her first term at college, when Hutt made her the indenture offer. In ten years she'd be free, and he'd settle money on her. The sum, to Caddie in the north woods, seemed like a fortune.

He was good about the money. Every month he and Caddie would ride over to the J.P. and Hutt would make his deposit and she would sign his receipt. And he never treated her as anything but a servant. She soon learned about his taste for bully truck drivers and army boys; so that was all right. She didn't mind the work, though it was hard and continuous; she did it with a kind of quick contempt that annoyed Hutt; apparently, he would have preferred her to be cheerful as well as efficient and strong. And once she had gotten a certain ascendancy over the routine, the work could be gotten away from. In every direction there were miles of unpeopled forests she could escape into, alone or with a pack horse, for days.

She learned that she had a talent for bearing things: not only heavy packs and cold nights and miles of walking, but also the weight of the days themselves, the dissatisfaction that she carried always like a pack, the *waiting:* for that's what she felt she was doing, always—waiting—and she convinced herself that it was the end of her ten years' indenture she waited for. But it wasn't.

The next morning was cold for September, which this far north meant nearly freezing. White steam rose from the pond, from the woolly pack horses Hutt kept for rent, and from the mounds of their droppings. When she went out to the goat shed, Caddie could see her breath, and steam rose too from the full milk pails. Everything warm, everything from the interior, steamed.

Coming back with the milk, she saw Ruta and Bonnie, the little pack horses, rearing and snorting, shunting each other against the corral walls. She came closer, calling their names, seeing now that their eyes were wide with fear. On the other side of the corral, the leo Painter leaned against the rail, smoking.

"What did you do to them?" she asked, putting down the milk. "Were you bothering them? What's wrong with you?"

"It's the smell," Painter said. His voice was thin, cracked, as though laryngitic.

"I don't smell anything."

"No. But they do."

How long could it have been since there was anything like a lion in these mountains? Last winter Barlo saw a bobcat, and talked about it for weeks. And yet maybe somewhere within Ruta and Bonnie the old fear lived, and could be touched.

"Trouble is," said Painter, "how are we going to use the damn animals if I scare them to death?" He threw down the cigarette with thick, golden-haired fingers. "We'll have a great time."

"We? Are you and Hutt going someplace?"

"Hutt?"

"Well, who do you mean, we?"

"You and me," Painter said.

She said nothing for a long moment. His face seemed expressionless, maybe because it wasn't completely human, or perhaps because he, like a cat, had nothing particular to express. Anyway, if he was making a joke, he didn't put it across. He only looked at her, steam coming from his narrow nostrils.

"What makes you think I'm going anywhere with you?" Caddie said. For the first time since she had seen Painter, she felt afraid of him.

He lit another black cigarette, clumsily, as though his hands were stiff with cold. "Last night I bought you. Bought your indenture from him—Hutt. You're mine now."

She only stared at him in disbelief. Then came a wave of anger, and she started up the muddy way toward the hotel, forgetting the milk pails. Then she turned on him. "Bought! What the hell does that mean? You think I'm a pair of shoes?"

"I'm sorry if I said it wrong," Painter said. "But it's all legal. It's in the papers, that he can sell the indenture. It's a clause."

He opened his stubby hand wide, and the flesh drew back from his fingertips to show curved white nails.

She stood, confused. "How can he do that? Why didn't he tell me?"

"You sold him ten years of your life," Painter said. "On time. He owns it, he can sell it. I don't suppose he even has to tell you. That's not in the papers, I don't think. Anyway, it doesn't matter."

"Doesn't matter!"

"Not to me."

She wanted to run to Hutt, hurt him, hit him, plead with him, hold him.

Ruta and Bonnie had stopped their shunting, and only snorted occasionally and huddled at the far side of the corral. For a while they all stood there, triangulated, the horses, Caddie, the leo.

"What are you going to do with me?" Caddie said.

✳

In the bar that night, Barlo and the two truck drivers stayed away from the table where Painter sat, though they glanced at him, one by one; he returned none of their looks.

The drivers had come up from the south. They wore uniforms of some kind, Caddie didn't know whose, their own invention maybe. They had the usual stories to tell, the refugees clogging the roads, the abandoned cars you had to avoid, the cities closed like fortresses. She had long ago given up trying to sort all that out. They had gone mad down there, had been mad since before she could remember anything. Painter's face showed no interest in them. But his ears did. His broad, high-standing ears were the most leonine, the most bestial, thing about his strange head. Partly hidden by his thick, back-swept hair, still they could be seen, pricking and turning toward the speakers with a will of their own. Perhaps he didn't even know they did so; perhaps it was only Caddie who saw it. She couldn't help glancing at him from behind the bar; her heart dove and rose again painfully each time she looked at him, sitting nearly immobile at his table.

"It don't matter to us," Barlo said. "We're independent anyways." This little chunk of north woods had seceded entirely, years before, and was now, officially, a dependency of Canada. "We got our own ways."

"That's all right," the elder driver said, "till they come to take you back again."

"The Fed," said the younger.

"Well, *I* ain't goin'," Barlo said, and grinned as though he had said something clever. "*I* ain't goin'."

Caddie was kept busy bringing beer for the drivers and rye for Barlo's coffee, and frying steaks, things Hutt usually did; but Hutt had gone over to the J.P.'s to get the papers notarized and a bill of sale made up: had left with a long angry mark on one cheek from Caddie's ring.

Until that morning, Caddie had thought she knew what shape the world had. She didn't like it, but she could stand it. She made it bearable by feeling little but contempt for it. Now, without warning, it had changed faces, expanded into a vertiginous gulf before her, said to her: the world is bigger than you imagined. Bigger than you can imagine. It wasn't only that Hutt had cheated her, and apparently there was nothing she could do about it, but that the whole world had: the fear and confusion she felt were caused as much by life betraying the quick bargain she had long ago made with it as by her finding herself suddenly belonging to a leo.

Belonging to him. No, that wasn't so. She washed glasses angrily, slapping them into the gray water. She belonged to no one, not Hutt, and certainly not this monster. She had never been owned; one of her constant taunts to her mother, trying to bring Caddie up respectably in spite of exile and poverty, had been, "You don't own me." Maybe once she had been owned by her father. Sometimes she felt a long-ago adhesion, a bond in her far past, to that man who grew vaguer in memory every year. But he had freed her by dying.

"Getting hot down in the N.A.," said the older driver. "Getting real hot."

"I don't get it," Barlo said.

"They're trying to put it all back together. The Fed. The

N.A.'s a holdout. Not for long, though. And if they join, where in hell will you be? They'll squeeze you to death."

"Well, we don't hear much up here," Barlo said uneasily. A silence occurred, made louder by the rattle of a loose window pane. The leo motioned to Caddie.

"I'd like some smokes."

The three at the bar turned to look at him, and then away again, as one. "We're out," Caddie said. "The truck won't come again till next week."

"Then we'll leave tomorrow," Painter said.

She put down the glass she had been wiping. She came and sat with Painter under the lantern, ignoring the alert silence at the bar. "Why me?" she said. "Why not a man? You could hire a man to do anything I can do, and more. And cheaper."

He reached over to her and raised her face to look at it. His palm was smooth, hard, and dry, and his touch was gentle. It was odd.

"I like a woman to do for me," he said. "I'm used to it. A man . . . it'd be hard. You wouldn't know."

Close to him, touched by him, she had thought to feel disgust, revulsion. What she felt was something simpler, like wonder. She thought of the creatures of mythology, mixed beasts who talked with men. The Sphinx. Wasn't the Sphinx part human, part lion? Her father had told her the story, how the Sphinx asked people a riddle, and killed everyone who couldn't solve it. Caddie had forgotten the riddle, but she remembered the answer: the answer was Man.

⁂

Hutt sat at a table near the door with his coffee, pretending to do his accounts. She passed him and repassed, bringing down Painter's gear from his room, dumping it onto the barroom floor, kitting it up neatly, and taking it out to the pack ponies.

"You're lucky, really," Hutt said. "These drivers said in a month, two months maybe, they'll close the highway. There'll be no more trucks. How would I pay you?" He looked at her as though for some forgiveness. "How the hell am I going to live?"

She only shouldered the last pack, afraid that if she tried to speak she wouldn't be able to, that the hatred she felt then for him would stifle her; she picked up Painter's carbine, which had an odd-shaped stock, and went out.

When Ruta and Bonnie were ready, Painter tried to take the lead rope, but Bonnie shied and tried to rear. Painter's lip curled, and he made a sound, a shriek, a roar, a sound that was all fierce impatience. He could have taken Bonnie's neck in one arm, but he seemed to gain some control of himself, and gave Caddie the rope. "You do it," he said. "You follow. I'll stay ahead or we'll never get there."

"Where?" she said, but he didn't answer, only took the carbine under his arm and started off with short, solid strides; as he walked, his shaggy head turned from side to side, perhaps looking for something, perhaps only from some half-instinct.

All that morning they went up the unfinished dirt truck road going north. The yellow earth-movers they passed were deserted, seemed to have been deserted for some time; apparently they had stopped trying to cut this road over the mountain. . . . From out of the constant forest sound there came a sound not quite of the forest, a dull, repeated sound, like a great quick watch. Ahead of her, Painter had stopped and was listening; he threw his head this way, then that. The sound grew more distinct, and suddenly he was running toward her, waving her off the road. "Why?" she said. "What's the matter?" He only made that harsh sound in his throat for answer, and pushed her down a crumbling embankment and into a tangle of felled trees and brush there. When Ruta and Bonnie pulled at the rope, reluctant to go down, he spanked them with his hand. The sound grew louder. Painter fingered his carbine, looking out from where they hid. Then, ghostly through the treetops, hovering like a preying dragonfly, a pale helicopter appeared. It turned, graceful and ominous; it seemed to quarter the area in its glance, as a searcher does. Then without a shift in its ticking voice it withdrew southward.

"Why did you hide?" she said. "Are they looking for you?"

"No." He smiled at her, something she hadn't known he could do, a slow and crooked smile. "But I wouldn't want them to find me. We'll go on now."

Mid-afternoon he had her make camp in a sheltered glade well off the road. "Eat if you want to," he said. "I won't today." He lay full-length on the heated ground pine, drawing up his muscled legs, resting his big head on his chin, and watching her work. She felt those lamplike eyes on her.

"I brought you cigarettes," she said. "I found a pack."

"Don't need them."

"Why did you say we had to leave when they were gone?"

"Men," he said. "Can't stand the smell. Not the men themselves, their places. The smell of, I don't know, their lives." His eyes began to close. "Nothing personal. The cigarettes block up the smell, is all." His eyes were slits; they closed entirely, then opened again. She had eaten and packed, and still he lay slipping in and out of sleep. Wherever it was he was going, he seemed in no hurry to get there.

"Lazy," he said, opening his eyes. "That's my trouble."

"You look comfortable," she said.

It would be many days before she understood that his direct, fierce stare more often than not looked at nothing; many days till in a fit of rage at being so intently regarded she stuck out her tongue at that gaze, and saw it drift closed without acknowledging the insult. He wasn't a man; he meant nothing by it.

Not a man. He was not a man. The men she had known, who had grasped and fumbled with her in a pleading, insistent way; the dark boy she had done the same with not long ago—*they* were men. Something leapt within her, at a thought she would not admit.

In the late afternoon he grew restless, and they went on. Perhaps by now the ponies had gotten used to him; anyway, they no longer shied from him, so Caddie could walk by his side.

"I don't want to pry," she said, even though she suspected irony would be lost on him, or perhaps because of that, "and you have the papers and all, but it'd be nice to know what's going on."

"It wouldn't," he said.

"Well," she said.

"Look," he said. "That copter we saw was looking for somebody. I'm looking for the same somebody. I don't know where

he is, but I've got an idea, and a better idea"—pointing up—
"than they have." He looked at her, expressionless. "If they find
him first, they'll kill him. If I find him first, they might kill both
of us."

"Both," she said. "What about me?"

He didn't answer.

What was it she felt for him? Hatred: a spark of that, a kind
of molten core at the center of her feelings that warmed the rest,
hatred that he had with so little thought snatched her from
where she had been—well, comfortable anyway. Hatred of her
own powerlessness was what it was, because he hadn't been
cruel. The uses he put her to were what she was for; it was in the
papers; there was no appeal from that and he made no bones
about it. He obviously couldn't put a polite false face on the
thing, even if it had occurred to him that it might make it easier
for her.

Which it wouldn't have. She knew her own story.

And yet in using her he wasn't like Hutt had been. Not constantly suspicious, prying, attempting to snatch from her every
shred of person she built for herself. No, he assumed her compe-
tence, asked for nothing more than she could do, said only when
they would stop and where they would go, and left the rest to
her; deferred, always, to her judgment. If she failed at anything
he never showed anger or contempt, only left her to patch up her
mistakes without comment.

So that slowly, without choosing to, resenting it, she became a
partner in this enterprise that she couldn't fathom. Had he consciously so drawn her into it? She supposed not. He probably
hadn't considered it that closely. *I like a woman to do for me,* he
had said. *You wouldn't know.*

And touched her cheek with his hard, dry palm.

"You cold?" he said. The fire had died to coals. Her own
sleeping bag was an old one, a grudging parting gift from Hutt.
She said nothing, trying not to shiver. "Damn, you must be.
Come over here."

"I'm fine."

"Come here."

It was a command. She lay coldly hating him for a while, but the command remained in the space between them, and at last she came, tiptoeing over the already rimy ground to where he lay large in his bag. He drew her down to him, tucked her efficiently within the cavity of his lean belly. She wanted to resist, but the warmth that came from him was irresistible. She thrust her damp cold nose into his furry chest, unable not to, and rested her head on his hard forearm.

"Better," he said.

"Yes."

"Better with two."

"Yes." Somehow, without her having sensed their approach, warm tears had come to her eyes, a glow of weeping was within her; she pressed herself harder against him to stifle the sudden sobs. He took no notice; his breathing, slow and with a burring undertone, didn't alter.

It was just light when she awoke. He had gone down to the quick stream they had camped by. She could see him, light-struck, the fine blond hair of his limbs glistening in the sun as though he were on fire. He was washing, delicately, carefully; and from within her cave of warmth she spied on him. Her heart, whether from the invasion of his privacy or from some other reason, beat hard and slow. He bent, drew up silver strands of water, and swept his hands through his mane; he rubbed himself. He bent to drink, and when he arose, droplets fell from his beard. When he came back to the campsite, drying himself with an old plaid shirt, she saw that above his long lopsided testicles his penis was sheathed, like a dog's, held against his belly by gold-furred skin.

From somewhere to the south the copter's drone could be heard briefly, like the first faint roll of a storm. He glanced up and hurried to dress.

Through that day, walking by him or ahead of him (for she was the better walker, she knew that now, his strength wasn't meant for endurance, or his legs not made for walking, yet he no longer stopped for long rests as he had before), she felt come and go a dense rush of feeling that made her face tingle and her breasts burn. She tried to turn from him when she felt it, sure that he could read it in her face; and she tried to turn away from

it herself, not certain what it was—it felt like clarity, like resolve, yet darker. Once, though, when he called out to her and
she was above him on a hard climb, she turned to face him, and
felt it rush up uncontrollably within her, as though she glowed.

"You're fast," he said, and then stood quiet, his wide chest
moving quickly in and out. She said nothing, only stared at him,
letting him see her, if he could; but then his unwavering gaze
defeated her and she turned away, heart drumming.

Late in the afternoon they came on the cabin.

He had her tie up the ponies in the woods well away from the
clearing the cabin stood in, and then for a long time watched the
cabin from the cover of the trees; he seemed to taste, carefully,
with all his senses, the gray, shuttered shack and its surroundings. Then he walked deliberately up to it and pushed open the
door.

"No one's been here," he said when she came into the shuttered dimness. "Not for weeks."

"How can you tell?"

He laughed shortly—a strange, harsh sound, little like a laugh
—and moved carefully through the two small rooms. In the afternoon light that filtered through the shutters she could see that
the place was well furnished—no logger's cabin, but something
special, a hideout, though from the outside it looked like any
shack. She went to open a shutter. "Leave that," he said. "Light
that fire. It's cold in here." He went from cupboard to cabinet,
looking at things, looking for something that in the end he didn't
find. "What's this?"

"Brandy. Don't you know?"

He put it down without interest.

"You were going to meet your somebody here."

"We'll wait. He'll come. If he can." The decision made, he
ceased his prowling. The fire, a bottled-gas thing, boomed when
she touched a match to it, and glowed blue. Why, she wondered,
bottled gas in the middle of the woods? And realized: for the
same reason that this place looks like a shack. Bottled gas makes
no smoke. No smoke, nobody home.

"Where are we?"

"A place."

"Tell me."

The heat of the fire had seemed to soften him. He sat on the small sofa before it, legs wide apart, arms thrown across its back. On a sudden impulse she knelt before him and began to unlace his boots. He moved his feet to aid her, but made no remark on this; accepted it, as he did everything she did for him. "Tell me," she said again, almost coyly this time, looking up at his big head resting on his chest. She smiled at him and felt a dizzy sense of daring.

"We are," he said slowly, "where a certain counselor, a government counselor, comes, sometimes, when he wants to get away say from the office or town, and where he might come if he had to get away from the government. And we'll meet him here. If we're lucky."

It was the longest speech she had ever heard him make. Without hurry she took off his boot and rolled the sweat-damp sock from his long, neat foot.

"What then?" she said, more to hear him talk than because she cared or understood; anyway, the blood sounding in her ears made it hard to think.

"This counselor," he said lazily, seeming not to care either, watching her unlace the stiff thongs of the other boot, "this counselor is a friend of ours. Of our kind. And his government wasn't. And his government down there has just collapsed, which you may or may not know, partly because he"—she drew off the other boot—"undid it, you could say, and so he's had to leave. In a hurry."

"Want some?" she said, showing him the brandy bottle.

"I don't know," he said simply. He watched her as she went around the room, finding glasses, breaking the bottle's seal; watched her, she knew, differently now. She felt a fierce elation, having embarked on this thing; felt the danger like the sear of the brandy. "Warm," she said, putting the glass in his hands, touching his fingers lightly. He raised the glass to his face and withdrew it quickly, as though it had bitten him; his nostrils flared and he put it down.

"How come—" she had not sat but walked now before him, holding her glass in two hands, past him and back again—"how come you don't have a tail?"

"Tails," he said, watching her, "are for four-legs. I'm a two-legs." His voice had darkened, thickened. "Couldn't sit down, with a tail. A piece of luck."

"I'd like a tail," she said. "A long, smooth tail to move . . ." She moved it. He moved. She moved away, a sudden voice urgent in her ears: *you can't do this you can't do this you can't do it you can't.*

He rose. The way he did it made it seem as though he was doing it for the first time after aeons of repose, the way movement gathered in his muscles to lift his heavy weight, the way his hands took hold of the couch to help him up; it was like watching something inanimate come frighteningly, purposefully alive in a dream. As he stood, his eyes somehow caught the fire's light and the pupils glowed brilliant red.

She was in a corner, holding her glass before her breasts protectively, her daring gone. "Wait," she said, or tried to say, but it was a sound only, and he had her: it was useless to struggle because he was helpless. She was swallowed up in his strength but he was helpless, taking her because he no longer had a choice: and she had done that to him. An enormous odor came from him, dense as an attar, mingling with the smell of spilled brandy; she could hear his quick breath close to her ear, and her trembling hand fumbled with his at her belt. Her heart was mad, and another voice, shrill, drowned out the first: *you're going to do it you're going to do it you're going to.*

"Yes," she said. She yanked at her belt. A button tore. "Yes."

She had thought that a single act of surrender was all she needed to make, that having made it she would be deprived of all will, all consciousness by passion, and that whatever acts followed would follow automatically. Her heat hadn't imagined difficulties; her heat had only imagined some swift, ineluctable coupling, like contrary winds mixing in a storm. It wasn't like that. He wasn't a man; they didn't fit smoothly together. It was like labor; like battles.

And yet she did find the ways, poised at times between repugnance and elation, to bare herself to him; drowned at times, suffocated at times in him as though he plunged her head under water; afraid at times that he might casually, thoughtlessly kill her; able to marvel, sometimes, as though she were another, at what they did, feeling, as though through another's skin, the coarse hair of his arms and legs, thick enough almost to take handfuls of. For every conjunction they achieved, there were layers of shame to be fought through like the layers of their thick clothing: and only by shameless strategies, only by act after strenuous act of acquiescence, her voice hoarse from exertion and her body slick with sweat, did she conquer them: and entered new cities, panting, naked, amazed.

She began to sob then, not knowing why; her legs, nerveless, folded under his careless weight. She lay against his thick thigh, which trembled as though he had run a mile. She coughed out sobs, sobs like the sobs of someone who has survived a great calamity: been shipwrecked, suffered, seen death, but against all odds, with no hope, has survived, has found a shore.

✳

She dreamed, toward dawn, curled against him, of muscle; of the tensed legs of his wives bearing him, of the fine bones and muscles of his hands, of her own slim arms wrapped in his, struggling with his. The soreness of her own muscles entered her dream, her own sinews tightening and slackening. She dreamed: *I did it I did it I did it.* She awoke exulting then for a moment and curled herself tighter against his deathlike sleep. She dreamed of his purring dreaming breath; it grew huge and menacing, and she awoke to the fast tick of the searching helicopter growing quickly closer. She moved to wake him, but he was awake already; all his senses pointed toward the growing sound. It became a roar, and its wind stirred in the cabin. It had landed outside.

He had a hand on her that she knew meant *keep still.* He turned, crouched and silent, toward the door, which was locked. Feet came across the pine needles toward the door with a sound they wouldn't have heard if they weren't all attention. Someone tried the door, paused, knocked, waited, pounded impatiently, waited again, then kicked in the door with a sudden crack. For a moment she could see a man silhouetted against the morning, could see him hesitate, looking into the shuttered gloom of the cabin, could see the gun in his hands. Then Painter, beside her, exploded.

She didn't see Painter move, nor did the one at the door, but there was a cry from his throat and a flurry of motion and he had seized the intruder, who made one sound, a sound Caddie would never forget—the desperate, shocked shriek of seized prey—and Painter had locked the man's head between his forearms. The man sank suddenly, as though punctured, his head loose on his body.

Painter, legs wide apart, supported him roughly—worried him, she would think later, like a cat, turning him this way and that to see if there was any life left in him—and then dropped him. "Sunless bastard," he said, or she thought he said. Beyond, in the tiny clearing, the copter's blades rotated lazily, not quite done.

✳

"Come in TK24," the radio said. "Come in TK24. Have you achieved O1?" It spoke in quick, harsh bursts, all inflection lost in an aura of static. Getting no reply from TK24 (who was dead), it began a conversation with someone else; the someone else's voice couldn't be heard, was pauses only, long or short. "Roger your request to return to base." . . . "No, that hasn't been verified as yet. He doesn't come in." . . . "Negative, negative. Listen, you'd be the first to know." . . . "That's what I understand. The cabin was his 01. Then the wrecked plane." A laugh, strangled in static. "Government. A real antique. He wouldn't get far." . . . "Positive, that is 02 of TK24 and we'll hear soon." . . . "Right, positive, over. Come in TK24, TK24 . . ."

On the glossy seat of the copter were charts covered with clear plastic. On one of them were circles in red grease crayon: one circle was labeled 01. The other circle, from what Painter could read of the map, was about ten miles off, up a sharp elevation, and was labeled 02.

Caddie came toward him, passing slowly the folded body of TK24, and feeling as though she had entered somewhere else, somewhere totally other, and had no way to get back. "You killed him."

"You're staying here," he said. "Up there on the mountain a plane's crashed. It might be him. If it isn't, I'll be back tonight or tomorrow."

"No."

"Get my rifle."

"I'll get it. But I'm coming with you."

He looked at her for a moment, looked at her—in a new way, with that new bond between them, looked—no. She felt a chill wave of something like despair. He looked the same. Nothing had changed, not for him. All her surrender had been for nothing, nothing. . . . He turned away. "Get the horses, then. We'll take them as far as we can."

If he wasn't made for walking, he was made less for climbing. Only his strength hauled him up, his strength and a fierce resolve she didn't dare break by speaking, except to tell him where she had found the easiest ways up. He followed. Once, she got too far ahead, lost sight of him, and couldn't hear him coming after her. She retraced her steps and found him resting, panting, his back against a stone.

"Monkey," he said. "A damned monkey. I haven't got your strength."

"Strength," she said. "Two hours ago you killed somebody, with your hands, in about ten seconds."

"I saw him first. It would've taken him even less. He had a gun." For the first time since he had turned those yellow eyes on her at Hutt's place the night she was being sold, she felt that he was trying to read her. "They want to kill us all, you know. They're trying."

"Who?"

"The government. Men. You." Still his eyes searched her. "We're no use to them. Worse than useless. Poachers. Thieves. Polygamists. We won't be sterilized. There's no good in us. We're their creation, and they're phasing us out. When they can catch us."

"That's not right!" She felt deep horror, and shame. "How can they . . . You've got a right to live."

"I don't know about a right." He stood, breaking his look. "But I am alive. I mean to stay that way. Let's go."

The government. Men. You. What did she expect from him, then? Love? The leo had bought her as men hunt leos. They were not one kind; never, never could she and he be one. He could only use her, or not, as he liked. She climbed fiercely, tears (of rage or pity, for herself or for him, she didn't know) breaking the chill morning into stars.

They found 02 fitted snugly into the trees at the end of a rocky pasture. Its wings were folded back, neatly, looking at rest like a bird's; but bits of the plane were scattered over the pasture violently, and its wings were never made to bend. Painter went near it cautiously. The long shadows of the forest crept across the field, quicker as the sun sank further. One crazed window of the plane flared briefly in the last sun. There was an absolute stillness there; the wrecked plane was incongruous and yet proper, like a galleon at the bottom of the sea. There was no pilot, dead or alive; no one. Painter stood by it a long moment, turning his head slowly, utterly attentive; then, as though he had perceived a path, he plunged into the woods. She followed.

He didn't go unerringly to the tree; it was as if he knew it must be there, but not exactly where it was. He stopped often, turned, and turned again. The long blue twilight barely entered here, and they must go slowly through the undergrowth. But he had it then: an ancient monarch, long dethroned, topless and hollow, amid upstart pines. Insects and animals had deposited the powdered guts of it at the narrow door.

"Good afternoon, Counselor," he said softly.

"If you come any closer," said a little voice within the tree, "I'll shoot. I have a gun. Don't try . . ."

"Gently, Counselor," Painter said.

"Is that you? Painter? Good god . . ."

She had come up beside him and looked into the hollow. A tiny man was wedged into the narrow space. His spectacles, one lens cracked, glinted; so did the small pistol in his hands.

"Come out of there," Painter said.

"I can't. Something's broken. My foot, somewhere." From fear, exposure, something, his voice sounded faint and harsh, like fine sandpaper. "I'm cold."

"We can't light a fire."

"There's a cell heater in the plane. It might work." She could hear in his voice that he was trembling. Painter withdrew into the trees toward the blue dimness of the pasture, leaving her alone by the tree. She squatted there, alert, a little afraid; whoever was looking for this counselor would come and find him soon.

"You don't," said the tree, "have a cigarette." It was a remark only, without hope; and she almost laughed, because she did: the pack she had put in her shirt pocket, for Painter, a lifetime ago. . . . She gave them to him, and her tin of matches. He groaned with relief. In the brief, trembling light of the match she glimpsed a long, small face, thick, short red hair, a short red beard. His glasses flashed and went out again. "Who are you?" he said.

"His." Yes. "Indentured, from now till . . ."

"Not a bit."

"What?"

"Against the law. No leo could possibly employ a man. You're not obliged. 'No human being shall be suborned by or beholden and subservient to a member of another species.'" A tiny bark of a laugh, and he relapsed into exhausted silence.

Painter came back carrying the heater, its element already glowing dully. He put it before the tree's mouth and sat; the tension had slipped from him like a garment, and he moved with huge grace to arrange himself on the ground. "Get warm," he said softly. "We'll get you out. Down the mountain. Then we'll talk." His eyes, jewellike in the heater's glow, drifted closed, then opened slowly, feral and unseeing.

"He said," Caddie said, "that you can't own me. In the law."

He could at that moment have been expressing rage, contempt, indifference, jealousy: she had no way to tell. His glower was as vast as it was meaningless. "Warm," he said. He scratched, carefully. He slept.

"Of course," said the little mocking voice inside the tree, "he is King of Beasts. Or Pretender anyway. But that never applied to men, did it? Men are the Lords of Creation."

Painter was a shaggy shape utterly still. The law. What could it matter? The bond between them, which she had made out of total surrender since she had no other tool to forge it with, couldn't be broken now; not even, she thought fiercely, by him. "I suppose," she said, "a person could stop being a Lord of Creation. Surrender that. And be a beast." There was a tiny hammer beating within her thigh where he had stretched her. She felt it flutter. "Only another beast of his."

"I don't know." He was moving within the tree, trying to extricate himself. "Of course he has always been my king. No matter how often I have failed him." A small cry of pain. "Or fooled him. Help me here."

She went to the tree and he held out for her to take an impossibly tiny black-palmed hand, its wrist long and fine as a bunch of sticks tied together. If he hadn't gripped her hard, like a little child, she would have dropped the hand in fear. He pulled himself toward the opening, and she could see his long mouth grinning with effort; his yellow teeth shone. "Who are you?" she said.

He ceased his efforts, but didn't release her. His eyes, brown and tender behind the glasses, searched her. "That's difficult to say, exactly." Was he smiling? She was close to him now, and an odor that before had been only part of the woods odor grew distinct. Distinct and familiar. "Difficult to say. But you can call me Reynard."

THREE

The flaying of Isengrim

The hardest work, Sten learned, was to carry the bird. Loren knew it was hard for a boy of fourteen to carry even a tiercel for the hours required, and he wore a glove, too, but Sten hated to give up the hawk; it was his hawk, he was the falconer, the hawk should be his alone to carry. If he rode, slowly, it was easier; but even on horseback Sten wanted desperately to lower his arm. Loren mustn't know that; neither must the hawk. As he rode, he spoke quietly, confidentially, to Hawk—he had never given him any other name, though Mika had thought of many: kingly, fierce names. Somehow, it seemed to Sten, any other name would be an excrescence, a boast about power and authority that a man might need but this bird didn't.

There had been a first frost that morning, and the leaves and brown grass they rode over were still painted with it; though the sun would be high soon and erase it, just for this moment it was lit with infinitesimal colored lights. Chet and Martha, the pointers, breathed out great clouds of frost as they studied the morning, padding with directness but no hurry toward the open fields that lay beyond the old stone farmhouse.

The farmhouse was mews, stable, and kennel, and Sten and Mika's private place. Their tutor, Loren, was allowed inside, but no one else. When their father had bought the long brown mansion whose roofs were still visible to them over the ridge, he'd wanted to pull down the old farmhouse and fill in the fulsome, duck-weedy pond. Sten had asked for an interview, and presented to his father the reasons for keeping them—for nature study, a place of their own to be responsible for, a place for the animals outside the house. He did it so carefully and reasonably that his father laughed and relented.

What his father had feared, of course, was that the place could be used for cover in an attack. The sensors around the grounds couldn't see through its walls. But he put aside his fears.

"Don't, Mika!" Sten hissed, but Mika had already kicked her bay pony into the proper gait. She took the low stone wall with great ease, gently, almost secretly, and quickly pulled up on the other side.

"Damn you," Sten said. His horse, seeing its cousin take off, had gotten restless to follow, and Sten had only one hand to settle him. Hawk bated on his wrist, the tassels of his hood nodding, his beak opening. He moved his feet on the glove, griping deeply; his bells rang. Furious, but careful, Sten picked his way through the fallen place in the wall. Mika was waiting for him; her brown eyes were laughing, though her mouth tried not to.

"Why did you do it? Can't you see . . ."

"I wanted to," she said, defensive suddenly, since he wasn't going to be nice about it. She turned her horse and went after Loren and the dogs, who were getting on faster than they.

It's Hawk, Sten thought. She's jealous, is all. Because Hawk is mine, so she's got to show off. Well, he *is* mine. He rode carefully after them, trying not to let any of this move Hawk, who was sensitive to any emotion of Sten's. Hawk was an eyas—that is, he had never molted in the wild; he was a man's bird, raised by men, fed by men. Eyases are sensitive to men's moods far more than are passage hawks caught as adults. Sten had done everything he could to keep him wild—had even let him out "at hack," after his first molt, though it was terrible to see him go, knowing he might not return to feed at the hack board. He tried to treat him, always with that gracious, cool authority his father used with his aides and officers. Still, Hawk was his, and Sten knew that Hawk loved him with a small, cool reflection of the passion Sten felt for him.

Loren called to him. Across the field, where the land sloped down to marshy places, Chet and Martha had stopped and were pointing to a ragged copse of bush and grapevine.

Sten dismounted, which took time because of Hawk; Mika held his horse's head, and then took up the reins. Sten crossed the field toward the place the dogs indicated, a thick emotion rising in him. When Loren held up his hand, Sten stopped and slipped Hawk's hood.

Hawk blinked, the great sweet eyes confused for a moment. The dogs were poised, unmoving. Loren watched him, and watched the dogs. This was the crucial part. A bad point from the dogs, a bad serve from Sten, and Hawk would lose his game; if he missed it, he would sit glumly on the ground, or skim idly around just above the ground, looking for nothing; or fly up into a tree and stare at them all, furious and unbidable; or just rake off and go, lost to them, perhaps forever.

Hawk shifted his stance on Sten's wrist, which made his bells sound, and Sten thought: he knows, he's ready. "Now!" he cried, and Loren sent the dogs into the bush. Hawk roused, and Sten, with all the careful swift strength he could put into his weary arm, served Hawk. Hawk rose, climbing a stair in the air, rose directly overhead till he was nearly as small as a swallow. He didn't rake off, didn't go sitting in trees; it was too fine a morning for that; he hung, looking down, expecting to see something soon that he could kill.

"He's waiting on," Mika said, almost whispered. She shaded her eyes, trying to see the black neat shape against the hard blue sky. "He's waiting on, look, look . . ."

"Why don't they flush it?" Sten said. He was in an agony of anticipation. Had he served too soon? Was there nothing in the copse? They should have brought something bagged. What if it was a grouse, something too big . . . ? He began to walk, steadily, with long steps, so that Hawk could see him. He had the lure in his pocket, and Hawk would have to come to that, if he would deign to, if . . .

Two woodcock burst noisily from the copse. Sten stopped. He looked overhead. Hawk had seen. Already, Sten knew, he had chosen one of them; his cutout shape changed; he began to stoop. Sten didn't breathe. The world had suddenly become ordered before his sight, everything had a point, every creature had a purpose—dogs, birds, horses, men—and the beautiful straight strength to accomplish it: the world, for this moment, had a plot.

Both the woodcock were skimming low to the ground, seeking cover again. Sten could hear the desperate beating of their wings. Hawk, though, fell silently, altering his fall as the cock he had chosen veered and fled. The other saw cover and dove into a brake as though flung there; the one Hawk had chosen missed the brake, and seemed to tumble through the air in avoidance, and it worked, too: Hawk misjudged, shot like a misaimed arrow below the woodcock.

Mika was racing after them. Sten, watching, had missed his stirrup and now clambered up into the saddle and kicked the horse savagely. Loren was whistling urgently to Chet and Martha to keep them out of it. The woodcock wouldn't dare try for cover again. It could only hope to rise higher and faster than the falcon, so the falcon couldn't stoop to it. The "field"—Sten, Mika, Loren on foot, and the dogs—chased after them.

Hawk rose in great circles around the climbing woodcock. Far faster and stronger, he outflew it easily, but must gain sufficient altitude for a second stoop. They were only marks in the sky, but their geometry was clear to Sten, who shaded his eyes with the big glove he wore, to see.

"He's beaten, look!" Loren cried. "Look!"

The woodcock was losing altitude, dropping, exhausted, raking off. Beaten in the air, it was trying for cover again, falling fatally beneath the hawk, who gathered above it. There was a line of trees at the pasture edge and the woodcock plummeted toward it; but it was doomed. Sten wondered, in a moment of cold clarity, what the woodcock felt. Terror only? What?

It was close to the line of woods when the falcon exploded above it, transforming himself, with a wing noise they could hear, from bullet into ax. His hind foot struck the woodcock with the certainty of a million generations, killing it instantly. He bore it to the ground, leaving a cloud of fine feathers floating in the path they had taken.

Sten came close carefully, his heart hard and elated, his throat raw from panting in the cold air. Hawk tore at the woodcock, a bleeding bolus of brown plumage, needle beak open. Sten stood over them and his mouth was suddenly full of water. He fumbled in his pocket for the lure. "Should I lure him off?"

"Yes," Loren said.

Hawk turned from breaking the cock's pinion to look up at Sten. He mantled, not wanting to rise to the fist, but greeting Sten; rejoicing, Sten tried not to think, in his master. Then he cocked his liquid eye at the woodcock, and with foot and beak returned to it. His bells made sounds as he worked. Unwillingly, not wanting to spoil Hawk's enjoyment, but knowing he must, Sten took out the lure. He looked to Mika where she held the horses, and to Loren, who watched the dogs. "Hawk," he said, all he could think to say. "Hawk."

On the ride home, he let Loren carry the falcon, because his arm had begun to tremble with the weight, but he walked nearby, leading his horse, letting Mika chase on ahead. When they came near the farmhouse, they saw Mika looking out to the weedy road that went past the house and farther on joined the gravel drive up to the mansion. A slim black three-wheeler had come off the road and was approaching. It slowed as it came near them, seemed to consider stopping, but then didn't. It picked up speed silently and turned onto the elm-shaded drive toward the mansion.

"Was that that counselor?" Mika asked.

"I guess," Sten said.

"What did he want here? Anyway, he's not allowed."

"Why not? Maybe he is. Isn't it only other people who can't come in? If he's not exactly people . . ."

"He's not allowed." For some reason, not cold, though her legs were bare beneath leather shorts, Mika shivered.

✳

The counselor wore an inverness cape because ordinary coats, even if they could be made to fit him, only emphasized his strangeness. His chauffeur opened the door of the three-wheeler's tiny passenger compartment and helped him out; he spoke quietly to the chauffeur for a moment and on tiny feet started up the broad stairs of the house, helping himself with a stick. The guards at the door neither stopped him nor saluted him, though they did stare. They had been instructed that it wasn't protocol to salute him; he wasn't, officially, a member of the Autonomy's government. They didn't stop him because he was unmistakable, there were no two of him in this world, and that also was why they stared.

Inside the mansion it was dim, which suited his eyes. He indicated to the servant who met him that he would retain cape and stick, and he was led down several halls to the center of the house.

Halls fascinated him. He enjoyed their odors of passage, their furniture no one ever used, their pictures not meant to be looked at—in this case, fox hunting in long-past centuries in all its aspects, at least from the hunter's point of view. He didn't mind when he was asked, with reserved apology, to wait for a moment in another hall. He sat on a hard chair and contemplated a black, sealed jar that stood on a—what? sideboard? commode? —and wondered what if anything it was pretending to be for.

The Director's appointments secretary, a woman of a certain lean nervosity common in powerful subordinates, greeted him without discernible emotion and led him through old, glossy double doors that had new metal eyes in them; past her own high-piled desk; across another metal thing set in the threshold of an arch; and into the Director's presence.

Hello, Isengrim, Reynard thought. He didn't say it. He made some conventional compliment, his voice thin and rasping like fine sandpaper drawn across steel.

"Thank you," the Director said, standing. "I thought it would be better to meet here. I hope I haven't inconvenienced you."

Jarrell Gregorius's voice was still faintly accented; he had learned English only as a schoolboy, when his father—whose portrait stood with the children's on an otherwise impersonally naked desk—came here with the international commission that had tried to arbitrate the partition. The commission had of course failed, though the idea of Autonomies remained, unlike as they were to the commission's complex suggestions. When the Malagasian member was kidnaped and executed, and it became obvious that the Autonomies were becoming, inevitably, disputing nations, the commission had disbanded, and Lauri Gregorius had gone home to ski, leaving them to their madness. Jarrell—Järl as he had been christened—stayed. The portrait on his desk was twenty years old.

"Will you take something? Lunch? A drink?"

"Early for both in my case."

"I'm sorry if we've called you too early."

Reynard sat, though the Director had not. It was among his privileges to be unbound by politenesses and protocol; people always assumed he couldn't understand them, didn't grasp the subtleties of human intercourse. They were wrong. "It's difficult to believe that any nocturnalism would have survived in me. But there it is. You can't have government solely at night."

"Coffee then."

"If convenient." He rested his red-haired tiny hands on the head of the stick between his knees. "I passed your children on my way up from the gate."

"Yes?"

"Someone, an adult, with them, with a bird on his wrist."

"A Mr. Casaubon. Their tutor."

"Beautiful children. The famous son resembles you as much as they say. Wasn't there a film . . ."

"A tape. I'm glad they're here now; the boy, I think, was beginning to be affected by the publicity. Here he can live a normal life."

"Ah."

"The girl has a different mother. Puerto Rican. She's only come to live here in the last—what?—eighteen months?" He had been pacing steadily in front of the tall windows seamed with metal that looked out toward raw concrete bunkers where men in Blue lounged. Gregorius would have looked well in Blue; its pure azure would have just set off his flawless, wind-burned skin and tawny hair. Instead, he wore black, noncommittal, well-tailored, somewhat abashing. "How," he said, "are we to behave today? Can we begin that way? The USE people will be here shortly."

"Will they bring the safe-conduct?"

"They say they will."

"And under what circumstances will they hand it over?"

"On receipt of a signed affidavit of mine endorsing the general aims of the Reunification Conference."

"As interpreted by USE."

"Of course."

"And you'll sign it?"

"I have no choice. USE's bargain with the Federal is that USE will accept the terms of reunification the conference arrives at, if USE can issue these safe-conducts."

"And since all the Autonomies must have representatives at the conference . . ."

"Exactly. They will arrive having, publicly at least, endorsed a USE view of reunification."

Reynard rested his long rufous chin on his hands, which held the stick between his knees. "You could refuse. Attempt to go down there without a safe-conduct . . ."

Gregorius stopped pacing. "Do you say that to test me, or what?" He picked up a small round steel box that lay on the desk and tapped its lid. "Without the safe-conduct I'd be detained at every border. With or without an armed guard. I certainly don't intend to battle my way down there." He opened the box, took a pinch of the glittering blue crystal it contained, and inhaled it. His eyes rested on his father's portrait. "I'm a man of peace."

"Well."

"I know," Gregorius said, "you're no friend of the Union for Social Engineering." He ran a hand through his proud hair. "You've kept me away from them. You were right. Those in the Directorate under their influence would have castrated me, with USE's help."

"But things have changed." Reynard could say such things without irony, without implication. It was a skill of his.

"*This* time," the Director said, "*this* time, reunification could work. Because of—well, my strength here, which you have helped me gain—I'm the logical choice, if a plan is arrived at, to direct. To direct it all." He sat; his look was inward. "I could heal."

Beyond the guardhouse the two children could be seen walking their horses; Gregorius looked out that way, but saw nothing, because, Reynard was astonished to see, his eyes glittered with tears.

*

Sten and Mika had begged one last ride before afternoon lessons began, and Loren had allowed it; he always did, the "one last" of anything, so long as it was truly the one last and not a ruse. That was their bargain, and the children mostly kept it.

"How can he be what you say?" Mika said.

"Well, he is. Loren said so."

"How." It was a command, a refusal, not a question.

"They made him. Scientists. They took cells from a fox. They took cells from a person . . ."

"What person?"

"What does it matter? Some person."

"It matters because that person would be his mother. Or his father."

"Anyway. They took these cells, and somehow they made a combination . . ."

"*Some*how."

"They *can!* Why do you want it not to be so?"

"I don't like him."

"Jesus. Some reason not to believe he's what he is. Anyway, they took the combination, is all, and they grew it up. And he came out."

"How could they grow it up? Loren says that deer and horses can't have children. Or dogs and foxes. How could a man and a fox?"

"It's not the same. It's not eggs and sperms. It's different—a mixture."

"Not eggs and sperms?" There was a sly, small laughter in her eyes.

"No." He had to keep this on a grown-up level. "A mixture—like the leos. You believe in them, don't you?"

"Leos. There are lots of them. They've got parents. And eggs and sperms."

"Now they do. But that's how they were first made: lions and
men. The counselor is the same, except he's new. How do you
think they first got leos?"

"Eggs and sperms," she said, abandoning reason, "eggsandsperms. Hey, Sperms. Let's play Mongol. Look!" She pointed
with her gloved hand. Down the hill, across another collapsing
stone wall—the vast property was seamed with them—they
could just see Loren, who had come out of the stone farmhouse
and was sweeping the yard with a great broom. He wore his long
coat of Blue, which he called his teacher shirt. "Look. A poor
peasant."

"Just gathered in his crop." He turned his horse. This was
their favorite game. It was a dangerous game; that was the only
kind Sten liked.

"Poor bastard," Mika said. "Poor eggsandsperms. He'll be
sorry."

"Burn the women and children. Rape the huts and outhouses."
He felt a lump in his throat, of laughter or ferocity he didn't
know. He banged his hard heels against the pony's flanks. Mika
was already ahead of him; she clutched her horse's bay ribs with
thighs muscled and brown (*"trigueña,"* she called the color:
"Nutlike," Loren translated; "Like a nut is right," Sten said).
She was streaking down on the wall; Sten would beat her to it.
He gave his Mongol yell and bent low over his careening horse.
The Mongol yell was a yell only, no words, sustained until his
breath gave out; when it did, Mika took up the yell, a higher,
clearer note with no male pubescent descant, and when she had
to stop he had begun again, so that the sound was continuous,
to keep Mongol spirits fierce and astound the cottagers. They
ran as close together as they dared, to make an army, almost
touching, the horses' feet a sound as continuous as their yell.

They took the wall together, Mika sitting neatly and
confident, Sten losing his hold for a frightening moment, the yell
knocked from him by impact. The farmer Loren looked up. He
had been carrying wood back into the farmhouse to get a fire
started for lessons, but he dropped it when he saw them and
dashed across the yard, coat flying, for the broom. He had it in
his hands when they rode down on him.

This was the scariest part, to ride hard right into the yard, without pulling up, as fast as they dared, as fast as the horses dared, coming as near as they dared to being thrown by the horses' excitement and as near as they dared to murdering the tutor they loved.

"Oh, no you don't," Loren shouted, "no you don't, not this year. . . ." He flailed with the broom at them, startling the horses, who wheeled around him, throwing up clots of farmyard, snorting.

"Give up, give up!" Mika cried, hoarse from yelling, striking at him with her little crop.

"Never, never, damn barbarians . . ." He was afraid, and afraid for the children, but not about to give in. He had to play as hard as they did. He gave Sten a swat on the shoulder with the broom, Sten's horse reared and wheeled, Mika laughed, and Sten went end-over onto the ground with a noise that brought a lump to Loren's throat.

"Peasants one, Mongols nothing," Loren said, rushing to Sten and holding him from getting up. "Wait a minute, let's see if any Mongol bones got broken."

"I'm all right." His voice was quavering. "Leamee alone."

"Shut up," Loren said. "Bend your legs up, slowly. All right, stand up. Bend over." He had to speak harshly, or Sten would cry, and hold it against him. "Oh, you're all right."

"That," Sten said with breathless dignity, "is what I said."

"Yes, all right." He turned to Mika. "Now the horses are good and lathered, are you happy?" She grinned down at him. "Go settle them down. And then let's go learn something." He pushed Sten toward the ramshackle stable. "Maybe next year, Genghis Khan."

"Loren," Mika said, "is that counselor what Sten says he is?"

"Tell her," Sten said, wanting this victory at least. "Once and for all."

"According to the journals of genetics, yes. If you mean is he half a fox, *vulpes fulva,* and half a man, *homo* sort of *sapiens,* whatever 'half' could mean in this context," he took a long breath, "yes."

"It's eerie." She slid from the saddle. "Why is he a counselor? Why does Daddy listen to him?"

"Because he's smart," Sten said.

Loren looked up to where the blank, bulletproof windows of the study could just be seen in the L of the house. "Yes, I suppose," he said, "or, as they used to say years ago, dumb like a fox."

✳

Reynard pushed his coffee cup away with a delicate, longwristed hand. "Supposing," he said carefully, "that the conference is a success. That reunification is somehow arrived at, or its beginnings anyway. I think you're right that you would be the choice to direct it. But if you went down under the auspices of the Union for Social Engineering, it would be their plan that you would direct, wouldn't it? I mean 'make the world work' and the rest of their ideas."

"I don't expect you to agree."

"What do you expect?"

"I don't want to be bullied by them. Of course I have to sign this statement. But I want to preserve some independence."

Reynard pretended to consider this. "Do this," he said at last. "Tell them today that you are preparing a statement of your own, a statement of goals for the conference. You want it included with theirs."

"They will refuse."

"Assure them it won't contradict theirs. That you will sign theirs if they will accept yours. If they refuse still, throw a rage. Announce their intransigence. Threaten to break off negotiations."

"None of that will do any good. They'll want capitulation."

"Of course. And in the end you'll capitulate."

"What have I gained? They'll say I'm hesitating, malingering."

"If they say that, admit it. It's true."

"But . . ."

"Listen. They know you are the only possible representative at the conference from this Autonomy. Let them know you require this measure of independence—a separate statement. If they

won't go that far, they will at least allow you to appear to negotiate for one."

"It seems like very little."

"You intend to sign. They know that."

Gregorius considered this, and his hand, which shook. "And
where is this statement? They won't wait long."

"I'll prepare it. Tomorrow you'll have it."

"I'd like to discuss it."

"No time. Believe me, it will be mild enough." He rose. The
appointments secretary, whose name was Nashe, approached.
"Did you know, by the way," Reynard said, "that USE has
recently developed a military arm?"

"Hearsay."

"Of course they are pacifist."

"I've heard the rumors."

"The USE people are here, Director," Nashe said.

"Five minutes," Gregorius said without looking at her.
"They've denied everything. Assassinations, terror bombings—
they've completely condemned all that, whenever they've been
linked with it."

"Yes. But the rumors persist." He took up his stick. "As effec-
tive, it seems to me, as if they were true. Now, is there another
exit here? I'd rather not pass the time with USE."

Gregorius laughed. "You amaze me. You hate them, but you
show me how to surrender to them."

"Hate," Reynard said, smiling his long, yellow-toothed smile,
"isn't the right word, exactly."

✳

When his counselor had sticked away without farewell,
Gregorius sat again in the deep chair behind the blank field of
his desk. He should compose himself for the USE people. They
would speak in that impenetrable jargon, dense as the priestly
Latinate of ancient Jesuits, though half of it was invented yesterday; would speak of social erg-quotients and a holocompetent
act-field and the rest of it, though what they wanted was clear
enough. Power. He felt, involuntarily, an apprehensive reflex:
his scrotum tightened.

That was why Reynard was invaluable. As invaluable as he was strange. He knew those ancient alterations of the spine and cortex, knew them when he saw them, though "saw" wasn't what he did. Unconfused by any intervening speech, he knew when a man was beaten, or unbeatable; he knew at what point fear would transmute within a man, alchemically, to anger. He had never been wrong. His advice must be taken. It had made Gregorius, and unmade his enemies.

Concerning USE, though, he couldn't be sure. How could a creature not quite a man tell Gregorius anything just, anything disinterested, about a force that wanted to make the world wholly man's? Perhaps at this point the fox ran out of usefulness to him.

And yet he had no choice. He no longer wholly trusted the fox, and yet there was no way now he could not follow his advice; he knew of nothing else to do. He felt a sudden rush of chemical hopelessness. The damn crystal. He looked at the silver cylinder on his desk, moved to pick it up, but did not.

He would be firm with them. It couldn't cost him anything to be intransigent for a day. It would be on record then that he was no thing of theirs to be slotted into their plans, or however they put it. He glanced at his watch. There would be no time today for his afternoon ride with Sten. He wondered if the boy would be disappointed. For sure he wouldn't show it.

"Nashe," he said in his beautifully modulated voice, "ask them to come in."

❋

There was no way for Reynard to conceive of himself except as men had conceived of foxes. He had, otherwise, no history: he was the man-fox, and the only other man-fox who had ever existed, existed in the tales of Aesop and the fables of La Fontaine, in the contes of medieval Reynard and Bruin the bear and Isengrim the wolf, in the legends of foxhunters. It surprised him how well that character fitted his nature; or perhaps, then, he had invented his nature out of those tales.

The guards at the gate neither stopped his black car nor saluted it.

The foxhunters (like those in the aquarelles that lined Gregorius's walls) had discovered long ago a paradox: the fox, in nature, has no enemies, is no one's prey; why, then, is he so very good at escape, evasion, flight? They used to say a fleeing fox would actually leap aboard a sheep and goad it to run, thus breaking the distinctive trail of it's scent and losing the hounds. The foxhunters concluded that in fact the fox enjoyed these chases as much as they themselves did, and used not natural terror in its flight but cunning practiced for its own sake.

And so they ran the fox to ground, and the dogs tore it to pieces, and the hunter cut off its face—its "mask," they used to say, as though the fox were not what it pretended to be—and mounted it on his hallway wall.

"What did he say?" the chauffeur asked when they were outside the grounds. "Will he give in to USE?"

"He will. Nothing I could say would move him."

"Then he'll have to die."

"Yes."

It had taken Reynard years to gather all the Directorate's power into Gregorius's hands, to eliminate, one by one, every other power center within the fluctuating, ill-defined government. When he was gone, the only person left in the Directorate capable of running the Autonomy would be the lean woman Nashe, who guarded his door.

Which is why, after years of self-effacing service, she had agreed to Reynard's plan.

She wouldn't, of course, last long. She was a servant only, however capable. She would fall, and there was no one else; factions only, like the crazy anarchist gang his chauffeur belonged to. There would be chaos.

Chaos. He couldn't, yet, deliver this realm in fealty to his king. He could bring to him, as fox Reynard did in the old tale, the skin of Isengrim the wolf. And make chaos. That was the best he could manage, and for the moment it would have to do.

Perhaps the old foxhunters hadn't been so wrong. A creature poised on some untenable line between predator and prey: that wouldn't be a bad school for cunning. For learning any art of preservation. For having no honor, none: not the innocence of prey, nor the predator's nobility. It was sufficient. If men wanted to create such a beast, he would be it; and he thanked them for at least having given him the means for survival.

"When do we get him?" the chauffeur asked.

"Tomorrow. When he rides out with the boy."

"We'll get the boy too."

"No. Leave the boy to me."

"We can't do that. He's too dangerous."

"I've given you your tyrant. Leave the boy to me, or we have no agreement." The chauffeur gave a suppressed cry of rage and struck the dashboard, but he said no more. Reynard found fanatics startling. Startling but simple: an equation, he might have said, had he understood anything but the simplest arithmetic, which he did not.

*

The tape about Sten that Reynard had seen had been immensely popular, had been shown continuously everywhere until its images had grown dim and streaky. It was as well known and worn as an old prayer, an old obeisance. Sten, a naked boy of eight or nine, a perfect Pan-god with flowers in his hair, leading folk to a maypole on donkeyback, laughing and happy in their adulation. Sten in stern black beside his father at some rally, his father's hand on his shoulder. Sten at the archery butts, careful, intent, somewhat overbowed, glancing now and again suspiciously into the recorder's eye as though its presence distracted him. Sten in Blue, playing with other boys; there seemed to be an aura around him, a kind of field, so that no matter how they all scrambled and chased together, the others always looked like his henchmen. The commentary was a praise-poem only. No wonder his father had tried to withdraw him from all this. "Sten Gregorius," it concluded, after describing his European ancestry, "son of a hundred kings."

Kings, Reynard thought. Kings are what they want. The desperate rationality of Directorates and Autonomies had satisfied no one; they wanted kings, to worship and to murder.

The day was colder. Afternoon seemed to be hurrying away earlier than it had yesterday. Through the deep windows of the farmhouse Reynard could see the moon, already risen, though the sun was still bright. A hunter's moon, he thought, and searched within himself for some dark response he was not sure would be there, or be findable if it were.

He wore no timepiece; he had never been able to correlate its geometry with any sense of time he felt. It didn't matter. He knew it was time, and though he doubted he would hear anything—should not, if his chauffeur and his comrades did their job right—his ears twitched and pointed with a will of their own.

He had never known a schoolroom, and its peculiar constellation of odors—chalk and children, old books and tape-players, pungency of an apple core browning somewhere—was new to him. He carefully pried into papers and fingered things. One of three butterfly nets remained in a rack. The other two, he knew, Mika and Loren had taken to a far pasture. He was glad of that. He felt capable of dealing with all three at once, but if he need not, so much the better.

He sat down on a hard chair with his back to a corner and rested his hands on his stick. He looked to the door just as it was flung open.

Sten, his chest heaving and his eyes wide, stood in the doorway with a drawn bow, its arrow pointed at Reynard.

"I'm unarmed," Reynard said in his small sandpaper voice.

"Someone's killed him," Sten said. His voice had a wild edge of shock. "I think he's dead."

"Your father."

"It was you."

"No. I've been to the house. I delivered a paper there. And came here to visit you." Sten's stare was fierce and frightened, and his arm that held the arrow had begun to tremble. "Tell me. Put down the bow. What was it that happened?"

Sten with a cry turned the bow from Reynard and released the arrow at full draw. It broke against a map of the old States, held with yellowing tape against the stone wall. He dropped the bow and fell, as much as sat, on the floor, his back against the wall. "We were riding. I wanted to go down to the beaver dam. He said he didn't have time, we'd just go the usual ride. We went through the little woods, along the wall." His face was blank now, affectless. "Why wouldn't he ride down to the dam?"

"He had no time." That noncommittal voice.

"There wasn't any sound. I didn't hear any. He just suddenly sat—straight up, and—" His face was suddenly distorted as a mental picture came clear. "Oh Jesus."

"You're quite sure he's dead." Sten said nothing. He was sure. "Tell me, then: Why did you come here? Why not to the house? Call the guard, call Nashe . . ."

"I was afraid." He drew up his knees and hugged them. "I thought they'd shoot me too."

"Well. They might have." A small elation began to grow in Reynard. He had taken a great chance, on slim knowledge, and it would work out. Knowing only Gregorius, and that tape—studying it, watching the boy Sten shrink from his father's hand on the podium, watching his self-possession, the self-possession of someone utterly alone—Reynard had learned that there was no love between Gregorius and his young heir. None. And when his father lay bleeding at his feet, dying, the boy had run, afraid for his own life: run not home for help but here. Here was home. "They still could." He watched fear, anger, withdrawal alternate within Sten. Alone, so terribly alone. Reynard knew. "Sten. What do you want now? Vengeance? I know who killed your father. Do you want to take up his work? You could, easily. I could help. You are much loved, Sten."

"Leave me alone."

"Is that what you want?"

For a long time Sten said nothing. He stared at Raynard, unable not to, and tried to pierce those lashless brown eyes. Then: "You killed my father."

"You father was killed by agents of the Union for Social Engineering. I know, because one of them was my chauffeur."

"Your chauffeur."

"He'll deny it. Say he had other reasons. But the evidence linking him to USE is there to be found, in his apartment in my house, which will doubtless be ransacked."

They were like Hawk's eyes, he thought at first, but they weren't. Behind Hawk's eyes were only clear intelligence and pitiless certainty. These eyes were watchful, wanting, certain only of uncertainty, and with a fleck of deep fear animating them. A mammal's eyes. A small mammal's eyes. "All right," he said at last. "All right." A kind of calm had come over him, though his hands had begun to shake. "You killed my father. Yes. I bet that could be proved. But you didn't kill me, and you could have." He prayed to Hawk: help me now, help me to take what I want. "I don't want anything from you, any of that vengeance or his work or any of that. I don't want your help. I want to be left alone. Let me stay here. They won't want to kill me if I don't do anything."

"No. I don't suppose so." He hadn't moved; he hadn't moved a red hair since Sten had opened the door.

"I won't. I swear it." A tremor had started in his voice, and he swallowed, or tried to, to stop it. "Give me the house and the land. Let me stay here. Let Mika and Loren stay too. The animals. It's all I want."

"If it is," Reynard said, "then you have it. No one but you could ever hold this land. Your mark is on it." No hint, no betrayal that this what he wanted from Sten, or even if such a plan had ever occurred to him. "And now I must flee, mustn't I? And quickly, since I no longer have a chauffeur; I'm a slow driver." He stood slowly, a tiny creature standing. "If you are careful, Sten, you need be neither predator nor prey. You have power, more maybe than you know. Use it to be that only, and you'll be safe." He looked around the stone place. It had grown dim and odorous with evening chill. "Safe as houses."

Without farewell, he left by the front door. Sten, still huddled by the back door, listened for the uncertain whine of the three-wheeler, and when it was gone, he stood. He had begun to shiver in earnest now. He would have to go up to the house, alert the guard, tell them what had happened. But not that he had come here: that he had stayed with his father, trying to stanch wounds . . .

Through the open door he could see, far off, Mika and Loren coming back across the field, Mika running, teasing Loren, who came carefully after with the collecting bottles. Their nets were like small strange banners. His only army. How much could he tell them? All, none? Would it have to be always his alone? Tears started in his eyes. No! He had to start for the house now, before they saw him, saw his horse.

He pulled up on the lawn before the white-stained perch where Hawk stood, preening himself, calm. In the growing twilight he looked huge; his great barred breast smooth and soft as a place to rest a baby's head.

How do you bear each day? Sten thought. How do you bear not being free? Teach me. How do you be leashed? Teach me.

✳

"Sten will stay quietly on that estate," Reynard said to Painter. "For a time, anyway. The Union for Social Engineering is being blamed for Gregorius's death, though naturally they will deny it strenuously. And my poor chauffeur, who probably hated USE even more than he hated Gregorius, will never get out of prison. The documents that made him a USE agent were put in his apartment by me. I gave USE good reason for murdering Gregorius: the paper I wrote for him, which of course he never saw, was a violent denunciation of USE, and contained some— rather striking—premonitions that taking this stand might cost him much. The paper will stand as the moving last words of a martyr to independence.

"The Reunification Conference won't be held. Not this year, not next. No one will trust USE any longer: an organization capable of butchering a head of state for disagreeing with it is no arbiter of peace and unity. I don't, however, put it past the Federal to try some other means of getting power in the Autonomy. There will be pretexts . . ."

Caddie listened to him with fascination, though she didn't understand much of what he said. It seemed as though he had only a certain store of voice, and that it ran out as he spoke, dwindling to a thin whisper; still he went on, talking about betrayals and murders he had committed without emotion, saying terrible ironies without a shade of irony in his voice. Painter listened intently, without comment. When Reynard had finished, he said only: "What good has it done me?"

"Patience, dear beast," Reynard whispered, leaning his delicate head near Painter's massive one. "Your time is not yet."

Painter stood, looking down at the fox. Caddie wondered how many men had ever seen them together so. Herself only? The oddness of it was so great as to be unfeelable. "Where will you go now?" Painter asked.

"I'll hide," Reynard said. "Somewhere. There's a limit to how far they can pursue me here, in this independency. And you?"

"I'll go south," Painter said. "My family. It's getting late."

"Ah." Reynard looked from Painter to Caddie and back again. "Just south of the border is the Genesis Preserve," he said. "Good hunting. No one can harm you there. Take that route." He looked at Caddie. "You?" he said.

"South," she said. "South too."

FOUR

*Go to the Ant, thou sluggard; consider her ways,
and be wise*

If they had lived on one of the lowest levels, the sun would already be setting for them; and down on the ground, only a few empurpled clouds would have been seen in a sky of lapidary clarity—if there had been anyone down on the ground to see them, and there wasn't, not for nearly a thousand square miles, which was the extent of Genesis Preserve. But up where they lived, above the hundredth level, they could still see the sun flaming crimson, and it wouldn't disappear from the highest terraces for minutes more. There was no other time when Meric Landseer felt so intensely the immense size of Candy's Mountain as when he looked down at evening into the twilight that extended over the plains, and watched it crawl level by level up toward him.

Sunlight pierced the glass he held, starting a flame in its center.

" 'You are the salt of the earth,' " Bree read, " 'and if the salt has lost its savor, wherewith shall it be salted?' What does that mean?"

"I don't know."

Bree sat upright on the chaise, her tawny legs wide apart, knees glossy with sun, with their extra share of sun. She scratched herself lazily, abstractly, turning the fine gold-edged pages. She was naked except for brown sunglasses and the thick gray socks she wore because, she said, her feet got cold first. The sun, striking lengthwise through the utter clarity of this air, drew her with great exactitude: each brown hair on her brown limbs was etched, every mole had highlight and shadow; even the serrations of her full, cloven lips were distinguished from the false wetness of the gloss that covered them.

Meric loved Bree, and she loved him, though perhaps she loved Jesus more. The sun made no distinctions, and in fact rendered the raw concrete of the terrace's edge as lovingly as it did the amber of Meric's drink or Bree's limbs. Jesus was unlightable; he made a darkness, Meric felt, fluorescing from the little book.

Shadow had climbed to their level. Bree put down the book. "Can you see them?" she asked.

"No." He looked out over the rolling grassland, fallow this year, that went on until evening swallowed it. Perhaps, if he had the eyes of the eagles who lived amid the clifflike roofs above, he could; he had watched the eagles, at his own terrace's height, floating on the complex currents, waiting for the movements of hares that undulated like fish in the sea of grass below. "No, I can't see them." Impossible for someone who lived here to fear heights, and Meric didn't; yet sometimes when he looked down a thousand feet he felt—what? wonder? astonishment?—some sudden emotion that waved him like a banner.

"It's cold," Bree said, almost petulant. A brief Indian summer had flamed and was going out again. Bree had taken it as a right, not a gift; she always felt wronged by the sun's departure. She stood, pulling a long robe of Blue around herself. Meric could look far down along the terraces that edged their level and see others, men and women, rising and drawing robes of Blue around themselves.

The sudden evening drop in temperature raised winds. The Mountain was designed not to intrude in any way upon the earth, to do no damage, none, to her body and the membrane of life stretched across it. Utterly self-contained, it replaced what it used of Earth's body exactly, borrowing and returning water and food by a nice reckoning. And yet the air was troubled by its mass; stuck up into the sea of air like an immense stirring-rod, it could raise and distort winds wildly. Once a year or so a vast pane of amber-tinted glass, faultily made, was sucked by wind from its place and went sailing out over the preserve for hundreds of yards before it landed. When that happened, they went out and found it, every splinter, and brought it back, and melted it, and used it again.

But they couldn't cease troubling the air. A building a half mile broad and nearly as high, set amid rolling hills of grass, will do that; and it was not only Meric who felt bad about that, and as it were begged Wind's pardon.

"They're there, though, aren't they," Bree said. She closed the terrace doors behind her, but a wind had gotten in and went racing around the level, lifting rugs and drapes of Blue and making the wall panels vibrate.

"They're there somewhere."

She turned up the tapers at the low table and nudged the pillows close to it with her gray-socked feet. Beyond their doorless space, far off perhaps—the drafts and airs made it hard to judge —men and women began an antique hymn as they returned from work; Meric and Bree could hear the tune but not the words.

"Your show begins again tonight, doesn't it," Bree said as Meric laid out their plain supper. "Does it mention them?"

"No. We didn't have tape or film. It wouldn't have done much good."

"People don't know what to think, though." She tucked the robe between her brown thighs and knelt Japanese-fashion before the table. "Should they be here?"

"They're not men."

"You know what I mean." The Preserve—the land that Candy's Mountain owned—was strictly forbidden to hunters, hikers, trespassers—men.

"I don't know. There was talk sometime of putting them on a reservation. They have to live."

"You feel sorry for them?" Bree asked.

"Yes. They're not men. They don't have freedom of choice, I don't think. They can't decide, like we can, not to . . . not to be . . ."

"Carnivores."

"Yes. Not to be what they are."

"We thank Thee, O Lord," Bree said, her long-lashed eyes lowered, "for these gifts Thou hast given us, which we are about to receive, in Jesus's name, amen."

She took bread, broke it, and gave it to him.

❋

When Meric had first come to live here, twenty years before, he was six years old and the great structure had not been inhabited for much longer than that. Its growth had begun to slow; it would never reach its two hundredth level. It would never, then, match exactly the exquisite model of it that Isidore Candy had made long before it had been begun. Among Meric's most deeply imprinted memories was his first sight of that model. In fact he remembered so little of his life before the Mountain—the fleeing, displaced life of refugees that burns an everlasting faint mark of insecurity on the soul but leaves few stationary objects in the mind—that it seemed as though his life began in front of that model.

"Look!" his mother said when their tiny, exhausted caravan was still miles away. "It's Candy's Mountain!" The enormous mass of it, blue with distance, rose like many great shoulders lifting themselves out of the earth; the skeleton shoulders of all the dead Titans coming forth together. Once it hove over the horizon, he saw it always no matter how the road they traveled twisted away from it; yet it was so big that it was a long time before they seemed to come any closer to it. It grew, and he must look always more sharply upward to see it, until they stood on the wide stairs of its threshold. The sea of grass they had crossed broke against those stairs in a foam of weed and flower, drowning the first tread, for no road or terrace led up to it. He stood on the stairs as though on a cliffy shore. When he tried to look up, though, the cliffs above were too huge to see. Around him, his people were mounting the stairs toward a hundred entrances that stood wide and waiting across the broken front; someone took his hand and he went up, but it was the Mountain itself that drew him in.

Their steps echoed in the vastest indoors Meric had ever seen or even dreamed of. The echoes had echoes, and those echoes fainter echoes. The whole arriving caravan was scattered across the chalky, naked stone of the floor, sitting on their bags or moving about, seeking friends, but they made no impression on the space, didn't diminish it at all. Yet at the same time its height and breadth were full of noises, people, activity, comings and goings, because the central atrium was strung all around with galleries, terraces, and catwalks: its depths were peopled, densely. Now that he was inside, it didn't seem to be a cliff on the seashore but the interior of the sea itself: life and movement, schools of busyness at every level.

He almost didn't dare to take steps there. There were so many directions to go, none marked and all seemingly infinite, that no decision was possible. Then a focus was given him: a girl, almost his age, in a dress of Blue, whose dark skin was like silk in the watery depths of this sunshot sea. She moved among the strangers as one who lived there, one of those who had taken the strangers in, one of those whom the weary, sad, desperate people he had traveled with wanted to become; and at that moment Meric wanted even more than that: he wanted to be her.

He hadn't ever quite stopped wanting that.

"Come see," she said to him, or at least to him and to others standing around him, grownups too distracted to hear her. He went with her, though, straight across the floor and into depths, following her. Beyond the central atrium, walls divided the space, bisecting it, halving and quartering it again and again as though he proceeded down some narrowing throat; and yet the heights and breadths remained, because most of these bisecting walls were transparent, an openwork of slats and suspended walks and cable-flown platforms, wood, metal, glass.

The place she brought him to, he knew now, years later, was in the very center of the Mountain. On a table there, standing nearly as high as himself, was the model of the Mountain. It was less like the model of a place than the idea of Place: space endlessly geometered by symmetries of lines, levels, limits. The sense grew only slowly in him that this was a model of the place he had come to live, that these dense accretions of closely set lines and serrated spaces modeled places large enough to live out lives in: were huge. The atrium he had stood stupefied in would not, in this model, have contained his fist; he could not have put a finger between the floors of any of the levels where multitudes lived and worked. Its tininess was the hugest thing he had ever seen. This, he thought, is how big it is. Its lines of wall and floor were made of materials whose fineness only made the idea of it grow bigger in his mind: gold wire and pins and grommets small as needles' eyes, steps made from single thicknesses of paper. Those steps he had mounted.

The girl pointed to a photograph suspended behind the model. An old man in a battered hat and a creased white shirt, with many pens in his shirt pocket; eyes kindlier than Santa Claus's and a beard like his too, which came almost to his waist.

"He built it," she said, and he knew that she meant both the model and in some sense single-handedly the place it was in as well. "His name was Isidore Candy. My name is Bree."

✳

Around them as they ate, Bree and Meric heard the endless, wordless voice of their level and, though too faint to be distinguished, of others too. The panels of paper that were all that made this space theirs, panels that in every size, height, and extent were all that made any space a space on this level, vibrated like fine drumheads to the voices, the gatherings of people, and the noises of work and machinery, a noise so constant and so multiform in its variations that they really didn't hear it at all; nor were they heard.

"How many are there?" Bree asked.

"Nobody's sure." He took more of the dense, crumbling bread. "Maybe ten or so."

"What is it they call it?" Bree said. "I mean a family of lions. Do they use the same word?"

"Pride," Meric said. He looked at Bree. There was in her brown, gold-flecked eyes an unease he couldn't read but knew; knew well though never how to make it pass. Was it fear? She didn't look at him. "A pride of lions. They use the same word."

She stood, and he suggested to himself that he not follow her with his eyes around the house ("house" they called it, as they called work-spaces "offices" and meeting-spaces "halls"; they knew what they meant). Something had been growing in her all day, he could tell it by her continual small questions, whose answers she didn't quite listen to.

Somewhere, clay bells rang, calling to meeting or prayer.

"Sodality tonight?" he asked. Why wasn't his tenderness a stronger engine against her moods?

"No."

"Will you come and see the show?"

"I guess."

He wasn't able not to look at her, so he tried to do so in a way that seemed other than pleading, though to plead was what he wanted to do; plead what, plead how? She came to him as though he had spoken, and stroked his cheek with the back of her hand.

Meric was so fair, his hair so pale a gold, that his sharp-boned face never grew a beard; his hair ran out along his ears like a woman's, and if he never shaved, a light down grew above his lip, but that was all. Bree loved that; it seemed so clean. She loved things she thought were clean, though she couldn't express just what "clean" meant to her. His face was clean. She had depilated herself because she felt herself to be cleaner that way. The softest, cleanest feeling she knew was when he gently, with a little sound like gratitude, or relief, laid his smooth cheek there.

She didn't want that now, though. She had touched him because he seemed to require it. She felt faintly unclean: which was like but different from feeling apprehensive.

She returned to her testament again, not as though to read it, but as though she wished to question it idly too. He wondered if she listened to Jesus's answers with any more attention than she did his.

"Why is it you want to know about them?" he asked. "What is it they make you feel? I mean when you think about them."

"I wasn't."

She perhaps wasn't. She might have meant nothing by her questions. Sometimes she asked aimless questions about his shows, or about technical matters he dealt with, tape, cameras. Sometimes about the weather. Maybe it was he who kept thinking about them; couldn't get the thought away from him. Maybe she only reflected an unease that he alone felt.

" 'Beware, watch well,' " Bree read, " 'for thine enemy like a roaring lion walketh about, seeking whom he may devour.' "

❋

The Birthday Show began this way:

Isidore Candy's hugely enlarged, kindly face, or his eyes, rather, filled the screens. The face moved away, so that his hat and great beard came into view. There was a rising note of music, a single note only, that seemed to proceed outward as the face retreated into full view. Through some art, the whole image was charged and expectant. A woman's voice, deep, solemn almost, said without hurry:

> *"There was an old man with a beard*
> *Who said: 'It is just as I feared.*
> *Two owls and a wren*
> *Three sparrows and a hen*
> *Have all built their nests in my beard.' "*

At that moment the single note of music opened fanwise into a breath-snatching harmony, and the image changed: The eagles who had aeries in the craggy, unfinished tops of the Mountain opened their ponderous wings in the dawn and ascended, one crying out its fierce note, their shaggy legs and great talons seeming to grasp air to climb.

It was a moment Meric loved, not only because he was almost certain of its effect, how it would poise the audience, at the show's beginning, on some edge between wit, surprise, awe, glory, warmth; but also because he remembered the chill dawn when he had hung giddy in the half light amid the beams, clutching his camera with numb fingers, waiting for the great living hulks within the stinking white-stained nest to wake and rise; and the joy in which his heart soared with them when they soared, in full light, in full view. He wasn't so proud of any image he had ever made.

The Birthday Show was all Meric's work. In a sense it was his only work: shown each year on Candy's birthday, it was changed each year, sometimes subtly, sometimes in major ways, to reinforce the effects Meric saw—felt, more nearly—come and go in the massed audiences that each year witnessed it. He had a lot of opportunity to check these reactions: even in the huge multiscreen amphitheater it took nearly a month of showings for everyone who lived in the Mountain to see it each year, and nearly everyone wanted to see it.

Bree thought of it as his only work, though she knew well enough that most of his year was taken up with training tapes, and a regular news digest, and propaganda for the outside. Those things were "shows." This was "your show." He asked her every year if she thought it was better now, and laughed, pleased, when she told him it was wonderful but she didn't notice that it was any different. She was his perfect audience.

Meric had acquired, or perhaps had by instinct, a grasp of the power a progress of images had on an audience, of the rhythms of an audience's perceptions, of what reinforcement—music, voice, optical distortion—would cause a series of random images to combine within an audience's mind to make complex or stunningly simple metaphors. And he made it all out of the commonest materials: though it was all his work, in another sense very little of it was, because he composed it out of scraps of old footage, discarded tapes, ancient documentaries, photographs, objects—a vocabulary he had slowly and patiently, with all the squirrelly ingenuity that had built Candy's Mountain itself, hoarded up and tinkered with over the years. The very voice that spoke to the audience, not as though from some pillar of invisibility but as though it were a sudden, powerful motion of the viewer's own mind, was the voice of Emma Roth, the woman he worked with in Genesis Section: a voice he had first heard speaking wildlife-management statistics into a recorder, a voice that made numbers compelling. A wizard's voice. And she completely unaware of it.

"Use it up," Emma's voice said in every ear, as they watched old tapes of the Mountain being built out of the most heterogeneous materials, "use it up, wear it out, make it do, do without": said no differently from the way she had said it one day to Meric when he asked about getting fresh optical tape. Yet she said it as though it were a faith to live by: as they did live by it.

Bree surrendered altogether to the mosaic of word and image, as she could surrender, at times, in prayer: in fact the Birthday Show was most like prayer. Some of it frightened her, as when over flaming and degraded industrial landscapes a black manna seemed endlessly to fall, and dogs and pale children seemed to seek, amid blackened streets, exits that were not there, and the sky itself seemed to have turned to stone, stained and eternally filthy, and Emma said in a voice without reproach or hope:

"The streams of Edom will be turned into pitch, and her soil into brimstone; her land shall become burning pitch. Night and day it shall not be quenched; its smoke shall go up forever. From generation to generation it shall lie waste; none shall pass through it for ever and ever. They shall name it No Kingdom There; and its princes shall be nothing."

For ever and ever! No, it could not be borne; Bree covered her mouth with her hands, hands ready to cover her eyes if she couldn't bear the scenes of war that followed: blackened, despairing faces, refugees, detention centers, the hopeless round of despair for ever and ever. . . . Only by stages was it redeemed; amaryllis in flower, cocoon opening, a butterfly's panting wings taking shape. Genesis Preserve: a hundred square miles stolen from Edom. Day rose over it, passed from it. She saw its fastnesses. Rapt, she let her hands slowly come to rest again. Emma spoke the words of an ancient treaty the Federal had made with the Indians, giving them the forests and plains and rivers in perpetuity, fine rolling promises; governments had made the same promises to the people of Candy's Mountain, and so there was warning as well as security in Emma's words. Then far off, seen from the unpeopled fastnesses of the Preserve, blue and shadowy as a mountain, remote, as though watched by deer and foxes, their home. Emma said again: "None shall ever pass through it for ever and ever; they shall name it No Kingdom There, and its princes shall be nothing," and Bree didn't know whether the change of meaning, which she understood in ways she couldn't express, made her want to laugh or cry.

Withdraw: that was what Candy had preached (only not preached, he was incapable of preaching, but he made himself understood, even as Meric's show did). You have done enough damage to the earth and to yourselves. Your immense, battling ingenuity: turn it inward, make yourselves scarce, you can do that. Leave the earth alone: all its miracles happen when you're not looking. Build a mountain and you can all be troll-kings. The earth will blossom in thanks for it.

A half century and more had passed since Candy's death, and still there was as yet only one of the thousand mountains, or setts, or coral reefs that Candy had imagined men withdrawing into for the earth's sake and for their own salvation. The building of that one had been the greatest labor since the cathedrals; was a cathdral; was its own god, though every year Jesus grew stronger there.

All the world's miracles: Meric had combed the patronizing nature-vaudevilles of the last century and culled from them images of undiluted wonder. There was never a time that Bree didn't weep when from the laboring womb of an antelope, standing with legs apart, trembling, there appeared the struggling, fragile foreleg of its child, then its defenseless head, eyes huge and wide with exhaustion and sentience, and the voice, as though carried on a steady wind of compassion and wisdom, whispered only: "Pity, like a naked newborn babe," and Bree renewed her vows, as they all silently did, that she would never, never consciously hurt any living thing the earth had made.

✳

Riding upward on the straining elevators, Bree felt that the taint of uncleanness was gone, washed away, maybe, by the sweet tears she had shed. She felt a great, general affection for the crowds she rode with; their patience with the phlegmatic elevator, the small jokes they made at it—"very grave it is," someone said; "Well, gravity is its business," said another—the nearness and warmth of their bodies, the sense that she was enveloped by their spirits as by breath: all this felt supremely right. What was the word the Bible used? Justified. That was what she felt as she rode the great distance to her level: justified.

She and Meric made love later, in the way they had gradually come most to want each other. They lay near each other, almost not touching, and with the least possible contact they helped each other, with what seemed infinite slowness, to completion, every touch, even of a fingertip, made an event by being long withheld. They knew each other's bodies so well now, after many years, since they were children, that they could almost forget what they did, and make a kind of drunkenness or dream between them; other times, as this time, it was a peace: it suspended them together in some cool flame where each nearly forgot the other, feeling only the long, retarded, rearising, again retarded, and at last inevitable arrival, given to each in a vacuum as though by a god.

Sleep was only a gift of the same god's left hand after these nearly motionless exertions; Bree was asleep before she took her hand from Meric. But, much as he expected sleep, Meric lay awake, surprised to feel dissatisfaction. He lay beside Bree a long time. Then he rose; she made a motion, and he thought she might wake, but she only, as though under water, rolled slowly to her side and composed herself otherwise, in a contentment that for some reason lit a small flame of rage in him.

What's wrong with me?

He went out onto the terrace, his body enveloped suddenly in wind, cold and sage-odorous. The immensity of night above and below him, the nearness of the sickle moon, and the great distance of the earth were alike claustrophobic, and how could that be?

Far off, miles perhaps, he could just see for a moment a tiny, clouded orange spark. A fire lit on the plains. Where no fire was ever to be lit again. For some reason, his heart leapt at that thought.

✻

In the mornings, Meric moved comfortably in seas of people going from nightwork or to daywork, coming from a thousand meetings and masses, many of them badged alike or wearing tokens of sodalities or work groups or carrying the tools of trades. Most wore Blue. Some, like himself, were solitary. Not seas of people, then, but people in a sea: a coral reef, dense with different populations, politely crossing one another's paths without crossing one another's purposes. He went down fifty levels; it took most of an hour.

"Two or three things we know," Emma Roth told him as she made tea for them on a tiny burner. "We know they're not citizens of anywhere, not legally. So maybe none of the noninfringement treaties we have with other governments applies to them."

"Not even the Federal?"

"It's all *men* that are created equal," Emma said. "Anyway, what can the Federal do? Send in some thugs to shoot them? That seems to be all they know how to do these days."

"What else do we know?"

"Where they are, or were yesterday." She was no geographer; the maps she had pinned to the wall were old paper ones, survey maps with many corrections. "Here." She made a small mark with delible pencil. Meric thought suddenly that after all no mark she could make would be small enough; it would blanket them vastly.

"We know they're all one family."

"Pride," Meric said.

Emma regarded him, a strange level look in her hooded gray eyes. "They're not lions, Meric. Not really. Don't forget that." She lit a cigarette, though the nearly extinguished stub of another lay near her in an ashtray. Smoking was perhaps Emma's only vice; she indulged it continuously and steadily, as though to insult her own virtue, as a leavening. Almost nobody Meric knew smoked; Emma was always being criticized for it, subtly or openly, by people who didn't know her. "Well," she'd say, her voice gravelly with years of it, "I've got so much punishment stored up in hell for me that one more sin won't matter. Besides" —it was a tenet of the cheerful religion she practiced—"what's all this fear of sin? If God made hell, it must be heaven in disguise."

Meric returned to the recorder he was trying to fix. It was at least thirty years old and incompatible with most of his other equipment, and it broke or rather gave out in senile exhaustion frequently. But he could make it do. "Are they, what do you call it, poaching?"

"Don't know."

"Somebody ought to find out." With an odd, inappropriate sense that he was tattling, he said: "I saw a fire last night."

"A lot of people did. I've had pneumos about it all day." With comic exactness, the tube at her side made its hiccup, and she extracted the worn, yellowed-plastic container. She read the message, squinting one eye against the smoke rising from her cigarette, and nodded.

"It's from the ranger station," she said. "They are poaching." She sighed, and wiped her hands on her coat of Blue as though the message had stained them. "Dead deer have been found."

Meric saw her distress, and thought: there are nearly a hundred thousand of us; there can't be more than a dozen of them. There are a thousand square miles out there. Yet he could see in Emma the same fear that he sensed in Bree, and in himself. Who were they that they could rouse the Mountain this way?

"Monsters," Emma said, as though answering.

"Listen," he said. "We should know more. I don't mean just you and me. Everybody. We should . . . I'll tell you what. I'll go out there, with the H5 and some discs, and get some information. Something we can all look at."

"It wouldn't do any good. They're poaching. What else do we need to know?"

"Emma," he said. "What's wrong with you? Wolves aren't poachers. Hawks aren't poachers. You're losing your perspective."

"Wolves and hawks," Emma said, "don't use rifles." She picked up the message. "Shot with old-style high-caliber ballistic weapon. Liver, heart removed, and most of the long muscle. Rest in a high state of decomposition."

Meric saw in his mind an image from the Birthday Show, a bit of some long-dead family-man's home movies, he assumed: hunters, laughing and proud, in antique dress, surrounded a deer, shot, presumed dead. The deer suddenly twitched, its eye rolling, blood gushing from its mouth. The men appeared startled at first; then one drew a long blade, and as the others stood near, brave beside this thing so nearly dead, he slashed the deer's throat. It seemed easy, like slashing a rubber bag. Blood rushed out, far more than seemed likely. Emma's voice said: "As ye do unto these, the least of my brethren, you do unto me." He'd always (however often, with repugnance, he passed this scene in his workprints) wondered what those men had felt: any remorse, any disgust even? He had read about the joy of the hunt and the capture; but that was over, here. Shame? Dread? That blood: that eye.

"Let me go," he said. "I'd be back in a week."

"You'd have to be careful. They're armed." She said the word as though it took courage to say, as though it were obscene.

"*Enemy* is a name for someone you don't know." It was a proverb of the Mountain's. "I'll be careful."

The rest of that day he prepared his equipment, making as certain as he could that it would function, working from a checklist of emergency spares and baling-wire (a term he used, without knowing what it had once meant, for little things he found useful for making repairs, making do). In the evening he went to visit friends, borrowing things to make up a pack. He took a scabbard knife.

He lay that night sleepless as well.

"It makes me nervous," Bree said to him. "How long will you be?"

"Not long. A week." He took her wrist, brown and smooth as a sapling. "I'll tell you what," he said. "If I'm not back in a week, send a pneumo to Grady. Tell him something's up, and to come on if he thinks it's right."

Grady was a ranger whom Bree had once had an affair with: brown as she was, but humorless, dense, as hard and reliable as she was evanescent. He was a member of the small, highly trained team in the Mountain allowed weapons—net-guns, tranquilizing guns, theoretically only for wildlife.

Wildlife.

"Grady would know," Bree said, and withdrew her wrist from his hand. She didn't like to be touched while she slept.

He'd often wondered what Bree and Grady had been for each

other. Bree had been frank about other lovers she'd had. About Grady, when he asked, she only said, "It was different," and looked away. He wanted to ask more, but he sensed the door shut.

He wanted to *see*. He wanted to enter into darkness, any darkness, all darkness, and see in it with sudden cat's eyes: nothing withheld. He realized, at the moment Bree took her wrist from him, that this was his nature: it was a simple one, but it had never been satisfied. Not so far.

✳

Genesis Preserve occupied a space in the northwest of the Northern Autonomy about where the heart would be in a body. The multilane freeways that cut it into irregular chambers were used now only by crows, who dropped snails onto them from heights to break the shells. Two hundred years ago it had been farms, hard-scrabble Yankee enterprises on a difficult frontier. Never profitable, the farms had mostly been given up by the beginning of the twentieth century, though the stone houses they had made by gleaning glacier-scattered fieldstone from their pastures remained here and there, roofless and barnless, home for owls and swallows. It had never ranked high in the last century's ephemeral vacation places: no real mountains to ski in the cruel winters, and an unlovely, barren upland in summer. Yet, by count, its swamps and variegated woods, its rocky fields and dense meadows harbored more varieties of life than did most equivalent cuts of earth. And it belonged to no one but them.

Meric was no outdoorsman. It was a skill few in the Mountain possessed, though many held it up as an ideal; it was thought to require a special kind of careful expertise, like surgery. He bore his time on the ground well, though; life in the Mountain was austere enough that short rations of dull food, cold nights, long walking didn't seem to be hardship. That was more or less how life was most of the time. And the solitudes, the sense that he was utterly alone in an unpeopled place that didn't want him there and would take no notice if, say, he fell down rocks and broke a leg, the hostility of night and its noises that kept his sleep fitful, all this seemed to be as it should. He had no rights in the Preserve: its princes, who protected it, were, when they entered it, nothing.

On the second day, toward evening, he came in sight of the pride.

He stayed well away, behind cover of a brush-overgrown wall, on a rise above where they had made camp. From his pack he chose a telephoto lens and, with an odd shiver as though the false nearness it gave him could make them somehow conscious of him as well, he began his spying.

They had chosen one of the roofless stone farmhouses as a base or a windbreak. Smoke from a fire rose up from within it. Around it were two or three carelessly pitched tents; a paintless and ancient four-wheel van; a kind of gypsy wagon of a sort he'd never seen before, and a hobbled mule near it, cropping. And there was an expertly made construction of poles and rope, a kind of gallows, from which hung, by its delicate hind legs, a deer. A doe. Focusing carefully, Meric could see the carcass turning very slowly in the breeze. There was no other movement. Meric felt the tense expectancy of a voyeur watching an empty room, waiting.

What was it that suddenly made him snap his head around with a stifled cry? Perhaps while his eyes were concentrating on the camp, other senses were gathering small data from his surroundings, data that added up without his being aware of it till an alarm went off within him.

Some fifty feet behind him a young male leo squatted in the grass, long gun across his knees, watching him steadily, without curiosity or alarm.

❋

"What is it you want?" Emma Roth said coldly, hoping to imply that whatever it was they wanted, they had no chance of getting it.

The three Federal agents before her, to whom she hadn't offered seats, looked from one to another as though trying to decide who should do the talking. Only the thin, intent one in a tight black suit, who hadn't produced credentials, remained aloof.

"A leo," one of them said at last, producing a dossier or file of some kind and exhibiting it to Roth, not as though he meant her to examine it, but only as a kind of ritual object, a token of his official status. "We have reason to believe that there is an adult male leo within the Preserve, who at one time called himself Painter. He's a murderer and a kidnaper. It's all here." He tapped the file. "He abducted an indentured servant north of the border and fled south. In the process he murdered—with his bare hands"—here the agent exhibited his own meaty ones—"an officer of an official Federal search party on other business."

"He murdered him on other business?" God, she hated the way they talked: as though it weren't they but some dead glum bureaucratic deity who spoke through them, and they were oracles only and had nothing to do with it.

"The officer was on other business," the agent said.

"Oh."

"We understand there is a formality to go through about getting safe-conducts or warrants to go into the Preserve and make an arrest. . . ."

"You don't understand." She lit a cigarette. "There are no formalities. What there is is an absolute ban on entering the Preserve at all, on whatever pretext. This is a protocol signed by the Federal and the Autonomy governments. It works this way: you ask permission to move onto the Preserve or enter the Mountain on what you call official business; and we refuse permission. That's the way it works." Twenty years of bribery, public pressure, and passive resistance had gone into those protocols and agreements; Roth knew where she stood.

"Excuse me, Director." The man in black spoke. It was a tight little voice with an edge of repressed fury in it that was alarming. "We understand about permission. We'd like to put in a formal request. We'd like you to listen to our reasons. That's what he meant."

"Don't call me Director," Emma said.

"Isn't that your title, your job description?"

"My name is Roth. And who are you?"

"My name is Barron," he said quickly, as though offering in return for her name something equally useless. "Union for Social

Engineering, Hybrid Species Project. I'm attached to these officers in an advisory capacity."

She should have known. The cropped hair, the narrow, careless suit, the air of being a useful cog in a machine that had not yet been built. "Well." The word fell on them with the full censorious weight of her great voice. "And what are these reasons."

"How much do you know," the USE man asked, "about the parasociety the leos have generated since they've been free-living?"

"Very little. I'm not sure I know what a parasociety is. They're nomads . . ."

With a dismissive gesture whose impatience he couldn't quite hide, Barron began to speak rapidly, his points tumbling over one another, stitched together with allusions to studies and statistics and court decisions Roth had never heard of. Out of the quick welling of his certainty, though, she did gather facts; facts that made her uncomfortable.

The leos' only loyalty was to their pride. Whether they had inherited this trait from their lion ancestors or had consciously modeled themselves on lion society wasn't known, because they felt no loyalty to the scientific community that had given them birth, and had freed them in order to study them, and so no human investigators were allowed among them to verify hypotheses. No human laws bound them. No borders were respected by them. Again, it was impossible to tell whether these attitudes were deliberate or the result of an intelligence too low to comprehend human values.

Smug, thought Roth: "an intelligence too low . . ." Couldn't it be a heart too great?

Given a small population, Barron went on, and the fact of polygamy and extended families, young leos find it difficult to mate. At maturity, they usually leave or are thrown out of the pride. Their state of psychic tension can be imagined. Their connection to the pride, their only loyalty, has been broken. Aggressive, immensely strong, subhuman in intelligence, and out to prove their strength in the world, the young leos are completely uncontrollable and extremely violent. Barron could give her instances of violent crime—crime rates among this population as compared to an equivalent human group, resisting arrest for instance, assaulting an officer . . .

"Is this one you're after," Roth broke in, "one of these young ones?"

"That hasn't been determined yet."

"He is one of a pride, you know." She wished instantly that she hadn't said that. The officers exchanged looks; Roth could tell that in fact they hadn't known. Yet why should she want to keep it secret? Only because the Mountain never gave away anything, no scrap even of information, to the outside society from which they took nothing? Anyway, it was out. "How did you come to learn he was in the Preserve?"

"We're not at liberty to say," said the USE man. "The information is reliable." He leaned forward, lacing his fingers together; his eyes rifled earnestness at her relentlessly. "Director, I understand that you feel deeply about the inviolability of your area here. We respect that. We want to help you preserve it. This leo or leos are in violation of it. Now, you're very peace-loving here"—a fleeting smile of complicity—"and of course we interface with you there, USE is of course strictly pacifist. So we feel that these leos, who as we've pointed out are all armed and violent, can't be handled by the means you have, which are peaceful and thus inadequate. The Federal government, then, is offering you aid in removing this violation of your space.

"Of course," he concluded, "you do want the violation removed."

For some reason, Emma saw in her mind Meric Landseer's long patient fingers moving with fine sensitivity to find the flaw in an old, well-loved, much-used machine.

"I might point out also," Barron said, since she remained silent, "that it's part of your agreement with the Federal not to turn the Mountain into a refuge for criminals or lawbreakers."

"We aren't hiding them," Roth said. "We can deal with them."

"Can you?"

On her desk the ranger memo still lay: *most of the long muscle stripped away, the rest in a high state of decomposition* . . . She lit a cigarette from the stub of her last. "There's no way," she said, "that I can issue warrants or passports in my own

name. You'll have to wait. It could take time." She looked at
Barron. "We're not very efficient decision-makers here." She
stood, strangely restless. She felt a hateful urgency, and wanted
it not to show. "I suppose it's possible for you to stay here for a
few days until our own rangers and—and other investigators
have returned with what they've learned. We have a kind of
guest-house." In fact it was a quarantine quarters, as cheerless as
a jail. That was fine with Roth.

Reluctantly, they agreed to wait. Roth began, with a slowness
that obviously irritated them, to send messages and fill out
passes. She thought: when bacteria invade you, you consciously
invade your own body with antibiotics. Neither is pleasant. An
ounce of prevention is worth a pound of cure. The pound of
cure before her accepted glumly their highly restricted passes.
Perhaps, possibly, thought Roth, the cure won't be needed. *Forgive us our trespasses,* she prayed, *as we forgive those who tres-
pass against us; lead us not into temptation, but deliver us from
evil.* . . .

✳

The creature Meric looked at was young. He couldn't have
said why that was apparent. He sat so calmly that Meric was
tempted to stand up and walk over to him, smiling. He hadn't
known what he would feel on coming close to a leo—he had
seen photographs, of course, but they were for the most part distant and vague and had only made him curious. He hadn't expected, then, that his first impression would be of utter, still,
unchallengeable beauty. It was an unearthly beauty that had
something suffocating in its effect, an alien horror; but it was
beauty.

"Hello," he said, smiling; both the little word and the fatuous
gesture fell hollowly far short of the leo, Meric felt. How could
he come to him? "I mean no harm." He was in fact harmless,
defenseless even. He wondered whether it was possible for him
to make himself clear to them. What if it wasn't? Why had he
supposed he would be invisible to them? What, anyway, had he
come out to learn?

The leo stood, and without prelude or greeting walked in short, solid strides to where Meric was crouched by the stone fence. He came with the unappeasable purposiveness of evil things in dreams, right at Meric, his intentions unreadable, and Meric, as in a dream, couldn't move or cry out, though he felt something like terror. He was about to fling his arms up before his face and cry out the nightmare-breaking cry, when the leo stopped and with an odd gentleness took the telephoto lens out of his hand. He looked at it carefully, batting a fly from before his face with a ponderous motion. Then he gave it back.

"It's nothing," Meric said. "A lens." The leo was close enough now for Meric to hear the faint whistle of air drawn regularly through his narrow nostrils; near enough to smell him. The smell, like the face, was alien, intensely real, and yet not anything he had expected: not monstrous.

"What did you want to see?" the leo said. At first Meric didn't understand this as speech; for one thing, the leo's voice was ridiculously small and broken, like an adolescent boy's with a bad cold. For another, he realized he had expected the leo to speak to him in some alien tongue, some form of speech as strange and unique as the creature itself.

"You," Meric said. "All of you." He began rapidly to explain himself, about the Preserve, about the Mountain, but in the middle of it the leo walked away and sat down on the stone fence, out of earshot. With his gun across his knees, he looked down the slope to where the camp lay.

Down there, where there had been no one before, there were leos. One, in a long loose coat like an antique duster, its head wrapped in a kind of turban, squatted by the door of the roofless farmhouse. Others—small, young ones apparently—came and went from her (why did he suppose the turbaned one to be female?). The young ones would run away together, playing, wrestling, and then return to her again and sit. She was passive, as though unaware of them. She appeared to be looking some way off. Once she shaded her eyes. Meric looked where she looked, and saw others: two more in long coats, carrying rifles resting upward on their shoulders, and another, behind them, in something like ordinary clothes, dressed like the young one who sat near Meric. One of the turbaned ones carried a brace of rabbits.

The leo on the wall watched them intently. His nostrils now and again flared and his broad, veined ears turned toward them. If he was intended to be a guard, Meric thought, he wouldn't be watching them; he'd be watching everything else. Not a guard, then. He seemed, rather, to be in some kind of vigil. Everything that happened down below absorbed him. But he made no move to go down and join them. He seemed to have forgotten Meric utterly.

Wondering whether it would be offensive to him, hoping it wouldn't, and not knowing how to ask, Meric put the lens to his eye again. The female by the door sat unmoving but attentive while the others came into camp. When they had come close enough to greet, though, no greetings were exchanged. The male —the one not in a long coat—came and sat beside her, lowering his great shape gracefully to the ground. She lifted her arm and rested it on his shoulder. In a moment they had so composed themselves that they looked as though they might have been resting like that for hours.

Meric moved his field of view slightly. Someone could be just glimpsed in the broken doorway; appeared partly and went away; came out then and stood leaning against the jamb with arms crossed.

It wasn't a leo, but a human woman.

Astonished, Meric studied her closely. She seemed at ease; the leos paid her no attention. Her dark hair was cut off short, and he could see that her clothes were strong but old and worn. She smiled at those coming in, though nothing was said; when the one with the rabbits dropped them, she knelt, drew a knife worn down to a mere streak, and began without hesitation to dress them. It was something Meric had never seen done, and he watched with fascination—the lens made it seem that he was watching something happening elsewhere, on another plane, or perhaps he couldn't have watched as the girl expertly slit and then tugged away the skin, as though she were undressing a baby who appeared skinny and red from within its bunting. Her fingers were soon bloodstained; she licked them casually.

The leo who sat near Meric on the wall stood. He seemed in the grip of a huge emotion. He started deliberately down the hill —they all seemed incapable of doing anything except deliberately—but then stopped. He stood motionless for a while, and then came back, sat again, and resumed his vigil.

Evening was coming on. The roofless house threw out a long tenuous shadow over the bent grass; the woods beyond had grown obscure. Now and again, clouds of starlings rose up and settled again to their disputatious rest. Their noise and the combing of the wind were all the sounds there were.

In an access of courage, feeling suddenly capable of it in the failing light, Meric stood. He was in their view now. One looked up, but started no alarm. Having then no choice—he had dived into their consciousness as a hesitant swimmer dives into cold water—he picked up his bag and started slowly but deliberately —in imitation, he realized, of their steady manner—down to the camp. He looked back at the leo on the wall; the leo watched but made no motion to follow or stop him.

✳

Night within Candy's Mountain was as filled with the constant sound of activity as was day. There was no time when the machine was shut down, for too much had to be done too continually if it was to stay alive at all. Great stretches of it were dark now; ways along halls were marked only by phosphorescent strips, signs, and symbols. Where more light was necessary, there was more light, but it was husbanded and doled nicely. Power in the Mountain was as exactly sufficient to needs, without waste, as was food.

Bree Landseer lay awake on her bedmat in the darkness. She needed no light and used none. She listened to the multiplex speak: the soughing of the hydraulic elevators, the crackle of a welding torch being used on the level above her, which now and then dropped a brief fiery cinder past her window. Voices: freak acoustics brought an occasional word to her, clear as those

sparks, through the paper partitions and drapes of Blue that
made her house: careful, brooms, novena, Wednesday, cup,
never again, half more, if I could . . . Where were those conver-
sations? Impossible to tell . . .

If there had ever been a human institution in which life had
been lived as it was within the Mountain, it wasn't any of the
ones that the outside world compared it to. It wasn't like a
prison, or a huge, self-involved family, or a collective farm, or
any kind of collective or commune. It wasn't like a monastery,
though Candy had known and revered Benedict's harsh and
efficient rule. Yet there was one institution it was like, perhaps:
one of those ancient Irish religious communities that never heard
of Benedict and only rarely of Rome, great and continuously
growing accretions of bishops, saints, monks, nuns, hermits,
madmen, and plain people all clustered around some holy place
and endlessly building themselves cells, chapels, protective walls,
cathedrals, towers. Yes, it was like that. In the Mountain no one
flogged himself daily or bathed cheerfully in brine for his soul's
good; but they had in the same way rejected the world for the
sake of their souls, while not the less—no, all the more—loving
and revering the world and all things that lived and flew and
crawled in it. They were as various and as eccentric here, as solitary, as individual, and as alone before God as those old Irish-
men in their beehive cells; and in the same way joined, too:
joined in a joyful certainty that they were sinners who deserved
their keep but no more. And as certain too that the world
blessed them for renouncing the world. Which saint had it been,
Bree wondered, who stood one morning in prayer with his arms
outstretched, and a bird came and settled in his hand; and so as
not to disturb her he went on praying; and so she made her nest
in his hand; and so he stood and stood (supported by grace) till
the bird had hatched and raised her young? Bree laughed to
think of it. A miracle like that would suit her very well. She
stretched her arms open across the rough cloth of the mat.

It was on nights like this that Meric and she, wrapped in the
delicate tissue of the Mountain's life-sounds, made their still
love. She opened the robe of Blue and touched her nakedness
delicately, following carefully to the end the long shivers that her

fingers started. Meric . . . Like grace, the lovely feelings were suddenly withdrawn from her. Meric. Where was he? Out there, in the limitless darkness, looking at those creatures. What would they do? They seemed to her dangerous, unpredictable, hostile. She wished—so hard it was a prayer—that Meric were here in the shelter of the Mountain.

She surrendered to the anxious tightening of her body, rolling on her side and drawing up her knees. Her eyes were wide open, and she listened to the sounds more intently now, searching them. And—in answer to her prayer, she was certain of it—she sorted from the ambience footsteps coming her way, the sound altering in a familiar way as Meric turned corners toward her. It was his tread. She turned over and could see him, as pale as a wax candle in the darkness of the house. He put down his bundles.

"Meric."

"Yes. Hello."

Why didn't he come to her? She rose, pulling the robe around her, and tiptoed across the cold floor to hug him, welcome him back to safety.

His smell when she took hold of him was so rank she drew back. "Jesus," she said. "What . . ."

He turned up the tapers. His face was as smooth and delicate as ever, but its folds and lines seemed deeper, as though filled with blown black dust. His eyes were huge. He sat carefully, looking around himself as though he had never seen this place before.

"Well," she said, uncertain. "Well, you're back."

"Yes."

"Are you hungry? You must be hungry. I didn't think. Wait, wait." She touched him, so that he would stay, and went quickly to make tea, cut bread. "You're all right," she said.

"Yes. All right."

"Do you want to wash?" she asked when she brought the food. He didn't answer; he was sorting through the bag, taking out discs and reading the labels. He ignored the tray she put before him and went to the editing table he kept in the house for his work. Bree sat by the tray, confused and somehow afraid. What had happened to him out there to make him strange like this? What had they done to him, what horrors had they shown him? He chose a disc and inserted it; then, with quick certainty, set up the machine and started it.

"Turn down the light," he said. "I'll show you."

She did, turning away from the screen, which was brightening to life, not certain she wanted to see.

A girl's voice came from the speakers: ". . . and wherever they go, I'll go. The rest doesn't matter to me anymore. I'm lucky . . ."

Bree looked at the screen. There was a young woman with short, dark hair. She sat on the ground with her knees drawn up, and plucked at the grass between her boots. Now and again she looked up at the camera with a kind of feral shy daring, and looked away again. "My god," said Bree. "Is she human?"

"No," the girl said in response to an unheard question. "I don't care about people. I guess I never liked them very much." She lowered her eyes. "The leos are better than people."

"How," Bree asked, "did she get there? Did they kidnap her?"

"No," Meric said. "Wait." He slid a lever and the girl began to jerk rapidly like a puppet; then she leapt up and fled away. There was a flicker of nothing, and then Meric slowed the speed to normal again. There was a tent, and standing before it was a leo. Bree drew her robe tighter around her, as though the creature looked at her. His gaze was steady and changeless; she couldn't tell what emotion it expressed: patience? rage? indifference? So alien, so unreadable. She could see the muscles of his heavy, squat legs beneath the ordinary jeans, and of his wide shoulders; at first she thought he wore gloves, but no, those were his own blunt hands. He held a rifle, casually, as though it were a wrench.

"That's him," Meric said.

"Him?"

"He's called Painter. Anyway, she calls him Painter. Not the others. They don't use names, I don't think."

"Did you talk to him? Can he talk?"

"Yes."

"What did he say?"

The leo began to move away from the tent door, but Meric reversed the disc and put him back again. He stood at the tent door and regarded the humans from his electronic limbo.

What had he said?

When Meric had gone down to where the leo stood broad and poised in the twilight, the leo hadn't spoken at all. Meric, in tones as pacific and self-effacing as he could make them, tried to explain about the Mountain, how this land was theirs.

"Yours," the leo said. "That's all right." As though forgiving him for the error of ownership.

"We wanted to see," Meric began, and then stopped. He felt himself in the grip of an intelligence so fierce and subtle that it made an apprehensive hollow in his chest. "I mean ask—see—what it was you'd come for. I came out. Alone. Unarmed."

The girl he had seen, and the females, had retreated into the shelter of the roofless farmhouse, not as though afraid but as though he were a phenomenon that didn't interest them and could be left for this male to dismiss. Someone within the walls was blowing a fire to life; spark-lit smoke rose over the walls. The young ones still played their silent games, but farther off. They looked at him now and again; stared; stopped playing.

"Well, you've seen," the leo said. "Now you can go."

Meric lowered his eyes, not wanting to be arrogant, and also not quite able to face the leo's regard. "They wonder about you," he said. "In the Mountain. They don't know you, what you are, how you live."

"Leos," said the leo. "That's how we live."

"I thought," Meric went on—it was exhausting to stand face to face like this, at a boundary, an intruder, and yet try to be intimate, carefully friendly, tentative—"I thought if I could just—talk with you, take some pictures, make recordings—just the way you live—I could take them back and show the others. So they could—" He wanted to say "make a decision about you," but that would sound offensive, and he realized at that moment that it was an impossibility as well: the creature before him would allow no decisions to be made about him. "So they could all see, you know," he finished lamely.

"See what?"

"Would you mind," Meric said, "if I sat down?" He took two careful steps forward, his heart beating hard because he didn't know just where he might step over some inviolable boundary and be attacked, and sat down. That was better. It gave the leo the superior position. Meric had made himself absolutely vulnerable, could be no threat here on the ground; yet he was now truly within their boundaries. He essayed a smile. "Your hunting went well," he said.

It would be a long time before Meric learned that such conversational ploys were meaningless to leos. Among men they were designed to begin a chat, to put at ease, to bridge a gap; were like a touch or a smile. The leo answered nothing. He hadn't been asked a question. The man had made a statement. The leo supposed it to be true. He didn't wonder why the man had chosen to make it. He decided to forget him briefly, and turned away into the enclosure, leaving Meric sitting on the ground.

Night gathered around him. He decided to remain where he was as long as he could, to grow into the ground, become ignorable. He took a yoga position he knew he could hold for hours without discomfort. He could even sleep. If they slept, and let him sleep here, in the morning he might have become a fixture, and could begin.

Begin what?

The girl touched him and he roused, uncertain for a wild moment where he was. There was a burnt, smoky odor in the air.

"Do you want to eat?" she said. She put a plate of brown chunks before him. Then she sat too, a little way off, as though uncertain how he might respond.

"It's meat," he said.

"Sure." She said it encouragingly. "It's okay."

"I can't."

"Are you sick?"

"We don't eat meat." A broken, blanched bone protruded from one brown piece.

"So eat grass," she said, and rose to go. He saw he had rejected a kindness, a human kindness, and that she was the only one here capable of offering him that—and of talking to him, too.

"No, don't go, wait. Thank you." He picked up a piece of the meat, thinking of her tearing it bloody from its skin. "It's just—I never did." The smell of it—burned, dark, various—was heady, heady as sin. He bit, expecting nausea. His mouth suddenly filled with liquid; he was eating flesh. He wondered how much he needed in order to make a meal. The taste seemed to start some ancient memory: a race memory, he wondered, or just some forgotten childhood before the Mountain?

"Good," he said, chewing carefully, feeling flashes of guilty horror. He wouldn't keep it down, he was certain; he would vomit. But his stomach said not so.

"Do you think," he said, pushing away his plate, "that they'll talk to me?"

"No. Maybe Painter. Not the others."

"Painter?"

"The one you talked to."

"Is he, well, the leader, more or less?"

She smiled as though at some interior knowledge to which Meric's remark was so inadequate as to be funny.

"How do you come to be here?" he asked.

"His."

"Do you mean like a servant?"

She only sat, plucking at the grass between her boots. She had lost the habit of explanation. She was grateful it was gone, because this was unexplainable. The question meant nothing; like a leo, she ignored it. She rose again to go.

"Wait," he said. "They won't mind if I stay?"

"If you don't do anything."

"Tell me. That one up on the hill. What's his function?"

"His what?"

"I mean why is he there, and not here? Is he a guard?"

She took a step toward him, suddenly grave. "He's Painter's son," she said. "His eldest. Painter put him out."

"Put him out?"

"He doesn't understand yet. He keeps trying to come back."

She looked off into the darkness, as though looking into the blank face of an unresolvable sadness. Meric saw that she couldn't be yet twenty.

"But why?" he said.

She retreated from him. "You stay there," she said, "if you want. Don't make sudden moves or jump around. Help when you can, they won't mind. Don't try to understand them."

Just before dawn they began to rise. Meric, stiff and alert after light, hallucinatory sleep, watched them appear in the blue, bird-loud morning. They were naked. They gathered silently in the court of the camp, large and indistinct, the children around them. They all looked east, waiting.

Painter came from his tent then. As though signaled by this, they all began to move out of the camp, in what appeared to be a kind of precedence. The girl, naked too, was last but for Painter. Meric's heart was full; his eyes devoured what they saw. He felt like a man suddenly let out of a small, dark place to see the wide extent of the world.

Outside the camp, the ground fell away east down to a rushy, marshy stream. They went down to the stream, children hurrying ahead. Meric rose, cramped, wondering if he could follow. He did, loitering at what he hoped was a respectful distance. As they walked down, he studied the strangeness of their bodies. If they were conscious of his presence, or of their own nakedness, they didn't show it; in fact they didn't seem naked as naked humans do, skinned and raw and defenseless, with unbound flesh quivering as they walked. They seemed clothed in flesh as in armor. A kind of hair, a blond down, as thick as loincloths between the females' legs, made them seem not so much hairy as cloudy. Walking made their muscles move visibly beneath the cloud of hair, their massive thighs and broad backs changing shape subtly as they took deliberate steps down to the water. In the east, a fan of white rays shot up suddenly behind down-slanting bars of scarlet cirrus, and upward into the blue darkness overhead. They raised their faces to it.

Meric knew that they considered the sun a god and a personal father. Yet what he observed had none of the qualities of a ritual of worship. They waded knee-deep into the water and washed, not ritual ablutions but careful cleansing. Women washed children and males, and older children washed younger ones, inspecting, scrubbing, bringing up handfuls of water to rinse one another. One female calmly scrubbed the girl, who shrank away grimacing from the force of it; her body was red with cold. Painter stood bent over, hands on his knees, while the girl and another laved his back and head; he shook his head to remove the water and wiped his face. A male child splashing near him attempted to catch him around the neck and Painter threw him roughly aside, so that the child went under water; Painter caught him up and dunked him again, rubbing his spluttering face fiercely. Impossible to tell if this was play or anger. They shouted out now and again, at each other's ministrations or at the coldness of the water, or perhaps only for shouting; for a spark of sun flamed on the horizon, and then the sun lifted itself up, and the cries increased.

It was laughter. The sun smiled on them, turning the water running from their golden bodies to molten silver, and they laughed in his face, a stupendous fierce orison of laughter.

Meric, estranged on the bank, felt dirty and evanescent, and yet privileged. He had wondered about the girl, how she could choose to be one of them when she so obviously couldn't be; how she could deny so much of her own nature in order to live as they did. He saw now that she had done no such thing. She had only acceded to their presence, lived as nearly as she could at their direction and convenience, like a dog trying to please a beloved, contrary, willful, godlike man, because whatever self-denial that took, whatever inconvenience, there was nothing else worth doing. Inconvenience and estrangement from her own kind were nothing compared to the privilege of hearing, of sharing, that laughter as elemental as the blackbird's song or the taste of flesh.

When they came back into camp they remained naked in the warming sunlight for a time, drying. Only the girl dressed, and then began to make up the fire. If she looked at Meric she didn't seem to see him; she shared in their indifference.

When he moved, though, there wasn't one of them who didn't notice it. When he went to his pack and got bread and dried fruit, all their eyes caught him. When he assembled his recorder, they followed his movements. He did it all slowly and openly, looking only at the machine, to make them feel it had nothing to do with them.

Painter had gone into his tent, and when Meric was satisfied that his recorder was in working order, he stood carefully, feeling their eyes on him, and went to the tent door. He squatted there, peering into the obscurity within, unable to see anything. He thought perhaps the leo would sense his presence and come to the door, if only to chase him off. But no notice was taken of him. He felt the leo's disregard of him, so total as to be palpable. He was not present, not even to himself; he was a prying eye only, a wavering, shuddering needle of being without a north.

"Painter," he said at last. "I want to talk to you." He had considered politer locutions; they seemed insulting, even supposing the leo would understand them as politeness. He waited in the silence. He felt the eyes of the pride on him.

"Come inside," Painter's thin voice said.

He took the recorder in a damp palm and pushed aside the tent flap. He went in.

＊

Bree looked at the screen. The sun shone through the fabric of the tent, making the interior a burnt-ocher color; the walls were bright and the objects inside dark, bright-edged, as though the scene were inside a live coal. The leo was a huge obscurity, back-lit. The recorder was wide open, so values were blurred and exaggerated; dust motes burned and swam like tiny bright insects, the leo's eyes were molten, soft, alive.

"You shouldn't have eaten that meat, Meric," she said. "You didn't have to. You should have explained."

Meric said nothing. The pressure of her ignorance on him, ignorance he could never dispel, was tightening around his heart.

"What do you want?" the leo said. For a long time there was no answer; the leo didn't seem to await one. Then Meric, faint, off-mike, said: "We think killing animals is wrong."

The leo didn't change expression, didn't seem to take this as a challenge. Meric said: "We don't allow it, anywhere within the Preserve."

Bree waited for the leo to make arguments, to say, "But all living things eat other living things"; or, "We have as much right to hunt as the hawks and the dragonflies"; or, "What right do you have to tell us what to do?" She had counterarguments, explanations, for all these answers. She knew Meric did too. She wanted to see it explained to the leo.

Instead the leo said: "Then why did you come out alone?"

"What?" Meric's voice, distant, confused.

"I said, why did you come out alone?"

"I don't understand."

"If you don't allow something, something I do, there ought to be more than one of you to make me stop."

As far as his emotions could be read, the leo wasn't being belligerent; he said it as though he were pointing out a fact that Meric had overlooked. Meric mumbled something Bree couldn't hear.

The leo said: "I have a living to get. It's got nothing to do with these—notions. I take what I need. I take what I have to."

"You have a right to that," Meric said. "As much as you need to live, I guess, but . . ."

The leo seemed almost to smile. "Yes," he said. "A right to what I need to live. That part's mine. And another part too for my wives and children."

"All right," Meric said.

"And another part as, what, payment for what I've gone through, for what I am. Compensation. I didn't ask to be made."

"I don't know," Meric said. "But still not all; there's still a part you have no right to."

"That part," the leo said, "you're free to take away from me. If you can."

Another long silence fell. Was Meric afraid? Bree thought, Why doesn't he say something? "Why didn't you *explain?*" she whispered. "You should have explained."

Meric pressed a lever on the editing table that froze the leo's unwavering regard, and the golden dust motes in their paths around him too. All along his long way home he had wondered how he would explain: to Bree, to Emma, to them all. All his life he had been an explainer, an expresser, a describer; a transformer, an instrument through which events passed and became meaningful: became reasons, programs, notions. But there was no way for him to explain what had happened to him in the leos' camp, because the event wouldn't pass through him, it would never leave him, he was in its grasp.

"I had nothing to say," he said to Bree.

"Nothing to say!"

"Because he's right." Right, right, how pointless. "Because if we want him not to do it, we have to make him. Because . . ." There was no way to say it, no way to pass it from him in words. He felt suffocated, as though he were caught in a vacuum.

When, after her affair with Grady, Bree had begun reading the Bible and talking and thinking about Jesus, she had tried to make Meric feel what she felt. "It's being good," she had said. Meric did his best to be good, to be Christlike, to be gentle; but he never felt it, as Bree did, to be a gift, a place to live, an intense happiness. He thought to say now that what he had felt in Painter's tent was what she had felt when she first knew Jesus, when she had glowed continually with it and been unable to explain it, when it made her weep.

But what could that mean to Bree? Her gentle Jesus, her lover who asked nothing of her but to stand with her and walk with her and lie down with her, what had he to do with the cruel, ravishing, wordless thing that had seized Meric?

"It's like Jesus," he said, ashamed, the words like dust in his mouth. He heard her breath indrawn, shocked. But it was true. Jesus was two natures, God and man, the godhead in him burning through the flesh toward his worshipers, burning out the flesh in them. Painter was two natures too: through his thin, strained voice pressed all the dark, undifferentiated world, all the voiceless beasts; it was the world Candy had urged us to flee from and Jesus promised to free us from, the old world returned to capture us, speak in a voice to us, reclaim us for its own. It was as though the heavy, earth-odorous Titans had returned to strike down at last the cloudy scheming gods, as though the circle had closed that had seemed an upward spiral, as though a reverse messiah had come to crush all useless hope forever.

As though, as though, as though. Meric looked up from the face on the screen, and drew a deep, tremulous breath. Tears burned on his dirty cheeks. The chains, as they had in Painter's tent, fell away from him. Nothing to say, yes, at last nothing to say.

Unable, despite a repugnance so deep it was like horror, to take her eyes from the screen, Bree heard unbidden in her mind the child's song she still sometimes sang herself to sleep with: *Little ones to him belong; they are weak but he is strong.* She shuddered at the blasphemy of it, and stood as though waking from an oppressive dream. "It doesn't matter," she said. "Pretty soon they'll be gone anyway."

"What do you mean?"

"Grady told me," she said. "There are Federal people here. One of those—animals committed a crime or something. The Feds want to go in and arrest him, or drive them off, or something."

He stood. She turned away from his look. "Grady's going with them. They were only waiting till you got back. What are you doing?"

He had begun to open cabinets, take out clothes, equipment. "I haven't come back," he said.

"What do you mean?"

He knotted together the laces of a pair of heavy boots so that they could be carried. "Do they have guns?" he asked. "How many are there? Tell me."

"I don't know. I guess, guns. Grady will be with them. It's all right." He seemed mad. She wanted to touch him, put a hand on him, restrain him; but she was afraid. "You have come back," she said.

He pulled on a quilted coat. "No," he said. "I came for this stuff." He was cramming recording tape, lenses, bits and pieces quickly into his pack. "I meant to stay a night, two nights. Talk to Emma." He stopped packing, but didn't look up at her. "Say good-bye to you."

A rush of fear contracted her chest. "Good-bye!"

"Now I've got to hurry," he said. "I've got to reach them before Grady and those." Still he hadn't looked at her. "I'm sorry,"
he said, quick, curt, rejecting.

"No," she said. "What's the matter?"

"I'm going back to them," he said. "I've got to—get it all
down. Record it all. So people can see." He slung the pack over
his shoulder, and filled his pockets with the bread she had set out
for him. "And now I've got to warn them."

"*Warn* them! They're thieves, they're killers!" She gasped it
out. "They don't belong here, they have to go, they have to *stop
it!*" He had turned to go. She grabbed at his sleeve. "What have
they done to you?"

He only shook her off, his face set. He went out of their space
and into the broad, low corridors that swept across the level.
From the long high lines of clerestory windows, bars of moon-
light fell across the ways. There was no other light. His footsteps
were loud in the silence, but her naked feet pursuing him made
no sound. "Meric," she whisper-called. "When will you come
back?"

"I don't know."

"Don't go to them."

"I have to."

"Let Grady."

He rounded on her. "Tell Grady to stay away," he said. "Tell
Emma. Don't let those men into the Preserve. They don't belong
there. They've got no right."

"No *right!*" She stopped, still, at a distance from him, as
though he were dangerous to approach. He stood too, knowing
that everything he had said was wrong, knowing he was doing
wrong to her, ashamed but not caring. "Good-bye," he said
again, and turned down a corridor toward the night elevators.
She didn't follow.

He went the night way down through the Mountain, following
the spectral luminescent signs, changing from elevator to elevator—the banks of day elevators were shut down, and there were
only one or two downward paths he could go; at every discharge
level he had to interpret the way to the next, drifting downward
side-to-side like a slow and errant leaf. How often he had

dreamed he walked through night spaces like these, coming onto unfamiliar levels, finding with surprise but no wonder places he had never seen, vast and pointless divisions of space, impassable halls, half-built great machines, processions of unknown faces, the right way continually eluding him and continually reappearing in a new guise—*oh now I remember*—until oppressed with confusion and strangeness he woke.

He woke: it seemed to him as he went down now that the Mountain had lost all solidity, had become as illusory as a thought, as a notion. The continual, sensible, long-thought-out divisions of its spaces, the plain, honest faces of its machines, its long black-louvered suntraps, its undressed surfaces, all showing the signs of the handiwork and labor that had brought them into being: it was all tenuous, had the false solidity of a dream. It couldn't contain him any longer, vast as it was.

He went out across the floor of the great, windy central atrium, past piles of supplies and materials—the place was never empty, always cluttered with things in progress from one condition into another under the hands of craftsmen, wood into walls, metal into machines, dirt into cleanliness, uselessness into use, use into waste, waste into new materials. Before him rose the transparent front, stories high, stone, steel, and pale green slabs of cast glass flawed and honest, through which a green, wrinkled moon shone coldly. He went out.

The moon was white and round. The grass before him bent, silvery, as it was mowed in long swaths by the wind. Behind him the Mountain was silent, a disturbance of the air only; its discreet lights didn't compete against the moon.

Certainty. That was what Painter offered him, only not offered, only embodied: certainty after ambivalence, doubt, uncertainty. He asked—no, not asked, could not ask; had no interest in asking, yet nevertheless he put the question—asked Meric to overthrow the king within himself, the old Adam whom Jehovah said was to rule over all creation. For even in the Mountain, King Adam was not overthrown, only in exile: still proud, still anxious, still throned in lonely superiority, because there was no new king to take up his abandoned crown.

That king had come. He waited out there in the darkness, his hidden kingship like a hooded sun. Meric had seen it, and had knelt before it, and kissed those heavy hands, ashamed, relieved, amazed by grace.

Give away all that you have, the leo said to men. Give away all that you have; come, follow me.

Meric stepped off the long steps into the whispering grass, not looking back, walking steadily north.

✳

They took Painter at the end of that month, a gray day and very cold, with a few snowflakes blowing in the air like dust. It had been Barron's plan to encircle the whole pride, if they could, and negotiate a settlement, taking the one called Painter into custody and arranging for the movement of the others, under supervision, southeastward in the general direction of the Capitol and the sites of the new internment centers. But the man Meric Landseer had spoiled that. He, and the young leo appearing from nowhere. It was to have been a simple, clean, just act, location, negotiation, relocation. It became a war.

The leos for a while seemed to be fleeing from them along the foothills of the mountains that formed the northern boundary of the Preserve. Barron decided that if the mountains were keeping them from moving north, he could swing some of his men quickly ahead of them and cut them off in a C-movement with the mountains blocking retreat. When they did that, though, the slow-moving caravan turned north suddenly, toward the steep, fir-clad slopes. Yet Barron had been told they didn't like mountains. It must be Meric Landseer influencing them.

There was a river, and beyond it a sudden mountain. They abandoned their truck and the wagon beside the river. They were gathering at the river's edge, about to cross, when Barron and the ranger showed themselves. The Federal officers were staying out of sight, guns ready. Barron called to the leos through a bullhorn, setting out conditions, telling them to put down their guns. There was no answering motion. The ranger, Grady, took the bullhorn from him. He called out Meric's name, saying he should stay out of this, not be a fool, get away. No answer. The females in their long, dull dusters were hard to see against the dull, brown grass.

Barron, talking peaceably but forcibly through the bullhorn, and Grady, carrying a heavy, blunt weapon like a blunderbuss, started to walk down toward the river. The leos were entering the water. Barron began to hurry. He supposed that the tallest of them, in ordinary clothes, was the one they wanted. He called on him by name to surrender.

He saw then out of the corner of his eye a quick figure moving in the woods to his left. Saw that he had a gun. A leo. Who? Where had he come from? Grady dropped instantly to the ground, pulling Barron down with him. The leo's gun fired with a dull sound, and then came a sharp chatter of fire from where the officers were hidden.

The young leo dodged from tree to tree, loading his ancient gun and firing. There was a shriek or scream from behind Barron: someone hit. Barron caught a glimpse of the leo now and then when he dared to raise his head. The bullhorn had fallen some feet away from him. He squirmed over to it and picked it up. He shouted that the leo was to throw down his gun, or the officers would shoot to kill. The leos were in the river now, wading chest-deep in its brown current, holding the children up. On the bank Painter still stood, and Meric, and another, the girl they had glimpsed during the chase, apparently the one he had kidnaped.

Suddenly the young one with the gun was racing, at an inhuman speed, out of cover, racing to put himself between the fleeing pride and the Federals. The guns behind Barron sounded. The leo fired blindly as he ran, and Barron and the ranger flattened themselves. He ran for a clump of bush. He seemed to stumble just as he reached it, then crawled to it, and fired again. The Federals covered the bush with fire.

Then there was a ringing silence. Barron looked up again. The young leo lay sprawled face up. The leo Painter had begun to walk alone away from the river toward where Barron and the ranger lay. He held a gun loosely in one hand. Barron thought he heard a faint voice, the girl's voice, calling him back. His hand trembling, Barron spoke through the bullhorn: put down the gun, no harm will come to you. The leo didn't look at the bush where the young one lay; he came toward them steadily, still holding the gun. Barron insisted he drop it. He said it again and again. He turned, and called out to the officers to hold their fire.

At last the leo threw down the gun, or dropped it, anyway, as though it were of no importance. At the river, the man was moving into the water with the girl, who was unwilling; she resisted, trying to turn back, struggling against the man, calling out to the leo. But the man made her go on. Some of the leos had already gained the far bank, and were climbing hand and foot up the fir-dark wooded slope. The ranger stood suddenly and raised his fat, blunt weapon.

He aimed well over the leo's head. The gun made a low boom, and instantly over the leo's head, like a hawk, there appeared a small amorphous cloud. There was a scream from the river, a girl's scream. The cloud flared open into a net of strong, thin cord, still attached to the gun by leads. It descended lazily, stickily, clingingly over the leo, who only as it touched him saw and tried to evade it. He roared out, pulling at the thing, and Grady at the other end hauled it tighter, shouting at the leo to relax, be quiet. The leo stumbled, his legs bound in the elastic cords. He was reaching for a knife, but his arms were enmeshed too tightly. He rolled over on the ground, the fine webbing cutting his face. Grady ran toward him and quickly, efficiently, like an able spider, made the cords secure.

Barron watched the two humans gain the opposite bank. The snow was still faintly blowing. What was wrong with them, anyway? Where did they think they were going?

He came to where the leo lay, no longer struggling. Grady was saying, "All right, all right," at once triumphant and soothing.

"What do you think you're doing?" Barron said to the leo. "What in *hell* do you think you're doing? I have a man dead here now." For some reason, shock maybe, he was furious. If the ranger hadn't been there, he would have kicked the leo again and again.

FIVE

Of the pack

Oh keep the Dog far hence that's friend to men
—T. S. Eliot

Blondie was dead.

They didn't understand that for a time; they stood guard over her hardening body, fearful and confused. She had been the first to eat the meat, though in fact it was Duke who had found it. He had sniffed it and taken a quick nip or two before Blondie had come up, imperious, knowing her rights, and Duke had backed away.

By rights, Sweets, as her consort, should have been next at the meat, before the real melee began, but something had alerted him, some odor he knew; he had made warning sounds at Blondie, even whimpered to get her attention, but she was too old and too hungry and too proud to listen. Duke was young and strong; he had had spasms, and vomited violently. Blondie was dead.

Toward nightfall, the rest began to drift away, tired of the vigil and no longer awed by Blondie's fast-fading essence, but Sweets stayed. He licked Blondie's stiff, vomit-flecked face. He did run a way after the others, but then he returned. He lay by her a long time, his ears pricking at sounds, lonely and confused. Now and again one of the wild ones came near, circling their old queen carefully, no longer sure of her status or Sweets's. They kept their distance when Sweets warned them off: he was still with her, she was still powerful, Sweets still shared that power.

But his heart was cold, and he was afraid. Not so much of the wild ones, who, fierce as they were, were so afraid of men and so timid about wandering beyond the park that they could never lead. No, not the wild ones. Sweets was afraid of Duke.

Sweets had smelled Duke's sickness and weakness; Duke was in no mood for any struggle now. He had gone off somewhere to hide and recover from the poison. Then there would be battle. Both of them, deprived of the queen who had kept peace between them, knew, in fitful heart-sinkings of insecurity, that their status was altered and that it must be established newly.

By dawn, Sweets had slept, and Blondie had grown featureless with frost. Sweets awoke conscious of one thing only: not Blondie, but the acrid odor of Duke's urine, and the near presence of the Doberman.

The struggle had begun. From around the park the pack had begun to assemble, all of them lean and nervous with the oncoming of winter, their calls carrying far on the cold air. They were of every size and color, from a dirty-white poodle not quite grown fully shaggy and with the filthy knot of a pink ribbon still in her topknot, to an aged Irish wolfhound, enormous and stupid. They each had a place in the pack, a place that had little to do with size or even ferocity, but with some heart they had or did not have. Places were of course eternally contested; only the old retriever Blondie had had no challengers. Between Sweets and Duke the issue was clear: who would be leader. For the loser, though, the battles would continue, until at least one other backed away from him and his place was found. It might be second-in-command. It could be, if his heart failed him, beneath the lowest of them.

If his heart failed him: when Sweets perceived Duke approach him, at once and in all his aspects, he felt a sudden overwhelming impulse to whimper, to crawl on his belly to the Doberman and offer himself up, to roll in and sniff up Duke's victorious urine in an ecstasy of surrender. And then quick as anger came another, fiercer thing, a thing that remade him all courage, that laid his teeth bare and drew back his ears, that erected his fur so that he appeared larger than his true size, that tautened his muscles and lashed him toward Duke like a whip.

*

Sweets's first pack had been a Chinese family on East Tenth Street, who had taken him milky and fat from his mother, the super's shepherd, and then put a sign on their door: PREMISES PROTECTED BY GUARD DOG. The whole block had been vacated by the provisional government shortly after that, before Sweets could yield up his whole allegiance to the shy, studious boy who was obviously the pack's leader. Sometimes, now, on garbage expeditions far south in the city, he would smell in the cans a faint odor of his earliest childhood.

The dogs on East Tenth Street who escaped the pound trucks were routinely shot by the paramilitary gangs, for hygienic reasons it was claimed, but chiefly so the boys could let off steam. Sweets had been among those impounded, and would have been destroyed with the rest of his snarling, terrified, famished cell if a fate in most cases usually worse hadn't befallen him: Sweets was one of those picked out by the laboratory of a city research center to see what he could teach them that might be of interest to the race that the race of dogs had taken as their leaders.

That was the first thing Sweets remembered, remembered that is not in his forgetless nerve and tissue but with the behind-his-nose, where he had come to locate his new consciousness: the laboratory of that research center. The ineluctable and eye-stabbing whiteness of its fluorescence. The bright metal bands that held him. The itching of his shaven head where the electrodes were implanted. The strong, disinfected, and indifferent hands of the black woman who, one day soon after his awakening, released him—let him walk, stiff and ungainly as a puppy, into the welcoming arms of his new mistress: "Sweets," she said, "sweets, sweets, sweets, come to mama."

The experiments Sweets had been used in were concerned with frontal-lobe function enhancement. They had been judged a failure. Sweets's EEG was odd, but there was no interpreting that; nobody trusted EEG anymore anyway, and Sweets had been unable to perform at all significantly on any test devised for him; apparently he had experienced no enhancement of func-

tion, no increase in eidetic intelligence. The whole line of research was being closed up as a mistake. And Sweets, having no
idea of what they were about, and altered in his mind only and
not in the soul he had inherited from the gray shepherd, his
mother, and the one-eyed mutt, his father, would not have
thought to tell them, even if he could speak, that he had awakened. He only wallowed, tail frantic, in the kindness of his lady,
a technician who had befriended him and claimed him when the
experiment was done. To her he gave up as much of his love as
had been left unshattered by his short life.

✻

It had taken centuries for the bonding of men and dogs to
come about, for dogs to come to accept men as of the pack. In
the city that bond was being unraveled in a mere decade.

It was fair that those species who had chosen to share city-
man's fate—dogs, cats, rats, roaches—should share in his
tragedies too, and they always had; the dogs willingly, the cats
with reproach, the rest blindly, starving with men, bombed with
them, burned out with them, sacrificed to their famines and their
sciences. But men had changed, quickly, far more quickly than
their companion species could. The rats, who had so neatly
matched man's filthy habits and who counted on his laziness,
had suddenly been done in by his wits, and had nearly perished
utterly: only now, in the loosening of man's hold over the world,
forgotten in the mental strife that only man can engage in, the
rats had begun to stage a small comeback: Sweets and his pack
knew that, because they hunted them. Cats had been rigidly
divided into two classes by the decline of the rat: sleek eunuchs
who lived long on the flesh of animals twenty times their own
size, fattened for them and slaughtered and cut into dainty bits;
and a larger class of their outcast cousins, who starved, froze,
and were poisoned by the thousand.

Until men left the city entirely, of course, the roaches would
flourish. But now, suddenly, that day seemed not far off.

Down Fifth from Harlem, the Renaissance fronts were stained
and their windows blinded with sheets of steel or plywood. The
park they had long regarded with calm possessiveness was rank

and wild, its few attendants went armed with cattle-prods, and their chief duty was to guard the concrete playgrounds kept open during daylight hours for children who played glumly with their watchful nurses amid the tattooed seesaws and one-chain swings. Few people went into the wilder park north of the museums, where ivy had begun to strangle the aged trees with their quaint nameplates, and city stinkweed to crowd out their young; few, except at need. "We lost them in the park," the provisional police would report after a street fight with one or another faction; lost them in the woods and rocky uplands where they hid, wounded sometimes, dying sometimes. The occasional police sweep through the park uncovered, usually, one dead or in hiding, and a number of scruffy, wary dogs, seen at a distance, never within rifle-range.

It was there that Sweets first saw Blondie: up beyond the museum, at the southern edge of her territory.

The open spaces around the museum were now a universal dog run, despite the police notices, since there were hardly any people who would go into the park without a dog. Sweets grew to know many, and feared some; dainty greyhounds who shied at squirrels, rigid Dobermans and touchy shepherds who knew only Attack and no other games, St. Bernards clumsy and rank. The dog run was a confusing, exhausting place, a palimpsest of claims all disputed. Sweets feared it and was excited by it; he strained at his leash, barking madly like a dumb puppy, when his lady Lucille first brought him there, and then when she unchained him he stood stock still, unable to leave her, assaulted with odors.

Whatever sense Sweets and the rest could make of the place was aborted by the people. Sweets should have had the weimaraner bitch; she was in flaming heat and shouldn't have been brought there, but since she had been, why had his first triumph, his first, over others larger and meaner than himself, been taken from him? The bitch chose him. He had never had a female, and his heart was great; he would have killed for her, and she knew it. And then the big-booted man had come up and kicked them away, and left Sweets in his triumph unrelieved.

Exalted, buzzing with power that seemed to spring from his

loins, he pranced away, hearing Lucille far away calling his name. They all faded behind him, and he was filled with his own smell only; he lowered his nose to the ground in a condescending way but nothing entered. He came to the top of the ridge, and in the bushes there Blondie rose up to meet him. He raised his head, not choosing to bark, feeling unapproachable, potent, huge, and she, though not in heat, acknowledged it. Bigger than he, she knew him to be bigger just then. She quietly, admiringly, tasted his air. And then lay down again to the nap he had roused her from, her tail making a soft thump-thump-thump on the littered ground.

*

And now Blondie is dead; murdered, he alone of them understands, by men's meat; and Lucille is gone, taken away unresisting in the night by big men in fear-smelling overcoats. Sweets, left locked in the bedroom, should have starved but did not, though Lucille in the relocation center wept to think of it; he knew well enough by then about doors and locks, and though his teeth and nails weren't made for it he opened the bedroom door, and stood in the ransacked apartment through whose open door came in unwonted night airs and odors.

He came to the park because there was nowhere else for him to go. If it hadn't been for Blondie, he would have starved that first winter, because he would no longer go near men, would never again look to them for food, or help, or any comfort. What the wild ones knew as their birthright, being born without men, he had as a gift of that eidetic memory men had given him by accident: he knew men were no longer of the pack. If he could he would lead his pack, all of them, away from men's places, somewhere other, though he had knowledge of such a place only as a saint has knowledge of heaven. He imagined it vaguely as a park without walls, without boundaries, without, most of all, men.

If he could . . .

When he rushed Duke, the Doberman didn't back away, though he himself didn't charge. His narrow, black face was open, his armed mouth ready. Duke had killed a man once, or helped to do it, when he was a guard dog in a jewelry store; the man's gun had shot away one of the ears the agency had so carefully docked when he was a pup. He feared nothing but noises and Blondie. He turned to keep facing Sweets as Sweets circled him in tense dashes, keeping the mouth facing him, wanting desperately to hurt him, yet unable to attack, which was Sweets's right.

When at last the courage within Sweets boiled over and he did attack, he was seized breathless by Duke's ferocity. They fought mouth to mouth, and Sweets tasted blood instantly, though he couldn't feel his cut lips and cheeks. They fought in a series of falls, like wrestlers, falls that lasted seconds: when Duke won a fall, Sweets would halt, paralyzed, offering his throat in surrender to Duke's wanting teeth, inches from his jugular. Then Duke would relent, minutely, and again they would be a blur of muscle and a guttural snarl, and Duke would be forced to freeze. Duke was the stronger: his nervous strength, teased up within him by his agency training, seemed ceaseless, and Sweets began helplessly—because he too had been doctored by men—to imagine defeat.

Then four sticks of dynamite took apart a temporary police headquarters on Columbus Avenue, and the sound struck them like a hand.

Duke twisted away, snapping his head in terror, seeking the sound to bite it. Sweets, surprised but not frightened, attacked again, drove Duke to yield; Duke, maddened, tried to flee, was made to yield again, and then lay still beneath Sweets, all surrender.

Sweets let him rise. He had to. He felt, irresistibly, an urge to urinate; and when he walked away to do so, Duke fled. Not far; from behind green benches along a walk he barked, letting Sweets know he was still there, still mean. Still of the pack. Only not leader.

Sweets, heart drumming, one leg numb, his lips beginning to burn in the cold air, looked around his kingdom. The others were keeping far from him; they were dim blurs to his colorless vision. He was alone.

❋

There were four officers and a single prisoner in the temporary station on Columbus Avenue. The prisoner was in transit from up north, where he had been captured, to a destination undisclosed to the officers, who were city and not Federal; all they knew was that he was to be held and transferred. And, of course, that a report had to be made out. It was this report, on six thin sheets of paper the colors of confetti, that the sergeant had been typing out with great care and two ringed fingers when he was decapitated by the file drawer—K–L—behind which the charge had been hidden and which shot out like an ungainly broad arrow when it went off.

"Height: 6′2″," he had typed. "Weight: 190." He didn't look it; slim, compact, but mighty. "Eyes: yellow." He could almost feel those strange eyes, behind him in the cell, looking at him. "Distinguishing marks." The sergeant was a methodical, stupid man. He pondered this. Did they mean distinguishing him from others of his kind, or from men? He had seen others, in films and so on, and to him they all looked pretty much alike. He wasn't about to get near enough to look for scars and such. The species had existed for nearly a century now, and yet few men— especially in cities—ever came as near to one as the sergeant was now. They were shy, secretive, close. And they were all marked for extinction.

The form just didn't fit the prisoner. The sergeant knew well enough what to do when, say, a man's name was too long for the space it was to be put in. He could guess weights and heights, invent the glum circumstances of an arrest. Distinguishing marks . . . He wrote: "Leo."

That certainly distinguished him. The sergeant used it twice more: in the Alias spot, and for Race. Pleased with himself, he was about to type it in for Nationality/Autonomy too, when the charge went off.

Two of the others had been in the foyer, and one was screaming. The third had been standing by the coffee urn, which was next to the cell door; he had been trying to catch a glimpse of their strange charge through the screened window. Now his head, face tattered by the screen, was thrust through the little window, wedged there, his eyes seeming to stare within, wide with surprise.

The leo shrieked in pain and rage, but couldn't hear his own voice.

✳

What had happened? The night streets north of Cathedral Parkway were always dead quiet on winter nights like this one; the loudest noises were their own, overturning garbage cans and barking in altercation or triumph; only occasionally a lone vehicle mounted with lights would cruise slowly up the avenues, enforcing the curfew. Tonight the streets were alive; windows rose and were slammed down again, loud sirens and bullhorns tore at the silence, red lights at the darkness. Somewhere a burning building showed a dull halo above the streets. There were shots, in single pops and sudden handfuls.

With Blondie gone, Sweets had no one to interpret this, no one who with certitude would say *Flee,* or *Ignore that, it means nothing.* It was all him now. The pack was scattered by incident over two or three blocks when mistrust overwhelmed Sweets. He began to lope along the streets, swinging his head from side to side, nostrils wide, seeking the others. When he passed one, the fear smell was strong; they were all of a mind to run, and had all begun to turn toward the long darkness of the park to the south. Sweets, though, kept circling, unsure, unable to remember whom he had passed and whom he had not. Duke, Randy, Spike the wolfhound, Heidi the little poodle, the wild ones Blondie's daughter and another one . . . He could bear it no longer. He turned to race across the avenue, meaning to go for the gate on 110th, when the tank turned the corner and came toward him.

He had never seen such a thing, and froze in fear in its path. Its great gun swiveled from side to side and its treads chewed the pavement. It was as though the earth had begun to creep. It churned a moment in one place, seeking with its white lights, which dazzled Sweets; then it started down on him, as wide almost as the street. It spoke in a high whisper of radio static above its thunderous chugging, and at the last moment before it struck him, there appeared on its top a man, popping up like a toy. Somehow that restored Sweets to anger; it was after all only another man's thing to hurt him. He leapt, almost quick enough; some flange of the tank struck him in the last foot to leave its path. He went sprawling and then rose and ran three-legged, ran with red fury and black fear contesting within him, ran leaving bright drops along the street until cold closed his wound. He ran uptown, away from the park; he ran for darkness, any darkness. This darkness: an areaway, a stair downward, a bent tin doorway, a dank cellar. And silence. Blackness. Ceasing of motion. Only the quick whine of his own breath and the roar of anger retreating.

Then his fur thrilled again. There was someone else in the cellar.

✳

Wounded beasts hide. It wasn't only that he, a leo, could never have passed unnoticed in the streets, certainly not coatless, and with an arm swollen, useless, broken possibly; not only that he knew nothing of the city. He had gone out into the streets still deafened by the blast, dazed by it; the street was dense with choking smoke. He began to hear people shouting, coming closer. Then the wail of sirens. And he wanted only and desperately silence, darkness, safety. The cellar had been nearest. He tore the sleeve of his coat with his teeth, so that the arm could swell as it liked; he tried not to groan when it struck something and the pain flooded him hotly. He sat all day unmoving, wedged into a corner facing the door, the pain and shock ebbing like a sea that could still summon now and again a great wave to rush up the shore of his consciousness and make him cry out.

Only when evening began to withdraw even the gray light that crept into the cellar did he begin to think again.

He was free. Or at least not jailed. He didn't bother to marvel at that, just as he hadn't marveled at the fact of being taken. He didn't know why the fox had betrayed them—and he was sure that was how it had come about, no one else knew that he was within the Preserve, no one else knew what he had done up north—but he could imagine one motive at least for Reynard:

his own skin. It didn't matter, not now, though when Reynard was before him again it would. Now what mattered was that he extract himself somehow from the city.

There was a river, he knew, west of here, and the only way out of the city was across that river. He didn't know which way the river lay; in any ordinary place he would have known west from east instantly, but the closed van they had brought him in, the blast, and the tangle of streets had distorted that sense. And if he knew how to find the river, he didn't know how to cross it, or if it could be crossed. And anyway, outside, the cruisers ran up and down the avenues and across the streets, making neat parallelograms around him endlessly: no path he knew how to find existed out there.

After nightfall, he began to hear the sounds of the reprisal against whoever it was that had bombed the station: the chug of tanks, the insistent, affectless voices of bullhorns. Guns. The sounds came nearer, as though bearing down on him. He drew the gun he had taken from a dead policeman; he waited. He felt nothing like fear, could not; but the steady rage he felt was its cognate. He had no reason to let them take him again.

When the dog growled at him, he snarled back instantly, silencing it. The dog could be theirs, sent to smell him out. But this dog reeked of fear and hurt, and anyway it wouldn't have occurred to Painter to shoot a dog. He put down the gun. As long as the dog made no noise—and if he was hurt and hiding, like Painter, he wouldn't—Painter would ignore him.

Sweets had thought at first: a man with a cat. But it was one smell, not two; and not a man's smell, only like it. He was big, he was hurt, he was in that corner there, but he didn't belong here—that is, this wasn't *his,* this cellar. Sweets knew all that instantly, even before his eyes grew accustomed to the place and he could see, by the gray streetlight that came through a high small window, the man—his eyes said "man" but he couldn't believe them—squatting upright in the corner there. Sweets retreated, three-legged, neck bristling, to a corner opposite him. He tried to lower his hurt leg, but when he put weight on it, pain seized him. He tried to lie, but the pain wouldn't allow it. He circled, whimpering, trying to lick the wound, bite the pain.

The small window lit whitely as a grinding noise of engines came close. Sweets backed away, baring teeth, and began to growl, helpless not to, answering the growl of the engines.

Men, he said, *men.*

No, the other said. *We're safe. Rest.*

The growl that had taken hold of Sweets descanted into a whimper. He would rest. The light faded from the window and the noise proceeded away. Rest . . . Sweets's ears pricked and his mind leapt to attention. The other . . .

The other still sat immobile in the corner. The gun hanging loosely in his hand glinted. His eyes, like a dog's, caught the light when he moved his head, and flared. Who is it?

Who are you? Sweets said.

Only another master of yours, the other said.

Sweets said: *No man is my master anymore.*

Long before you followed men, the leo said, *you followed me.*

(But not "said": not even Painter, who could speak, would have told himself he had been spoken to. Both felt only momentary surprise at this communication, which had the wordless and instant clarity of a handshake or a blow struck in anger.)

I'm hurt and alone, Sweets said.

Not alone. It's safe here now. Rest.

Sweets still stared at him with all his senses, his frightened and desperate consciousness trying to sort out some command for him to follow from the welter of fears, angers, hopes that sped from his nose along his spine and to the tips of his ears. The smell of the leo said, Keep away from me and fear me always. But he had been commanded by him to rest and be safe. His hurt leg said, Stop, wait, gather strength. The rivulets of feeling began, then, to flow together to a stream, and the substance of the stream was a command: Surrender.

Making as much obeisance as he could with three legs, he came by inches toward the leo; he made small puppy noises. The leo made no response. Sweets felt this indifference as a huge grace descending on him: there would be no contention between them, not as long as Sweets took him for master. Tentatively, nostrils wide, ready to move away if he was repulsed, he licked the big hand on the leo's knee, tasting him, learning a little more of the nature of him, a study that would now absorb most of his life, though he hadn't seen that yet. Unrepulsed, he crept carefully, by stages, into the hollow between Painter's legs, and curled himself carefully there, still ready to back off at the slightest sign. He received no sign. He found a way to lie down without further hurting his leg. He began to shiver violently. The leo put a hand on him and he ceased, the last of the shiver fleeing from the tip of his tail, which patted twice, three times against Painter's foot. For a time his ears still pricked and pointed, his nostrils dilated. Then, his head pressed against the hard cords of Painter's thigh and his nose filled with the huge, unnameable odor of him, Sweets slept.

Painter slept.

The sounds of a house-to-house search coming closer to where they hid woke them just before dawn.

Nowhere safe then, Painter said.

Only the park, Sweets said. *We'll go there.*

(It wouldn't happen often between them, this communication, because it wasn't something they willed as much as a kind of spark leaping between them when a charge of emotion or thought or need had risen high enough. It was enough, though, to keep the lion-man and the once-dog always subtly allied, of one mind. A gift, Painter thought when he later thought about it, of our alteration at men's hands; a gift they had never known about and which, if they could, they would probably try to take back.)

They went out into a thin dawn fog. Sweets, quick and afraid, still limping, stopped whenever he found himself outside the leo's halo of odor, paced nervously, and only started off again when he was sure the other followed. He lost the way for a time, then found traces of the pack, markings, which were to him like a man's hearing the buzz and murmur of distant conversation: he followed, and it grew stronger, and then the stone gateposts coalesced out of the fog. Between them a black shape, agitated, called out to him, unwilling to leave the grounds but pacing madly back and forth: Duke! Sweets yipped for joy and ran with him, not feeling the pain in his leg, snapping at Duke, sniffing him gladly, and stopping to be sniffed from head to toe himself and thus tell of his adventures.

Duke wouldn't come near the leo; he stood dancing on the lip of the hill while Sweets and Painter went slipping down the wet rotten leaves and beneath the defaced baroque bridge and through the dank culvert into the safety—the best safety Sweets knew—of their most secret den, where no man had ever been, where his wild ones by Blondie had been born and where she had tried, dying, to go.

Yours now, he said, and the great animal he had found fell gratefully into the rank detritus of the den, clutching his hurt arm and feeling unaccountably safe.

✳

Winter had begun. Sweets knew it, and Painter. The others only suffered it.

One by one they had come to accept Painter as of the pack, because Sweets had. At night they gathered around him in the shelter of the den, which was in fact the collapsed ruins of a rustic gazebo where once old men had gathered to play cards and checkers and talk about how bad the world had grown. There was even a sign, lost somewhere in the brake of creeper and brush, which restricted the place to senior citizens. The pillars that supported it had failed like old men's legs, and its vaulted roof now lay canted on the ground, making a low cave. The pack lay within it in a heap, making a blanket of themselves. Painter, a huge mass in the middle of them, slept when they did, and rose when they rose.

He and Sweets provided for the pack. Painter had strengths they didn't have, and Sweets could hunt and scavenge as well as any of them, but he could think as well. So it was they two who were the raiders. They two executed the zoo robbery, which yielded them several gristly pounds of horsemeat intended for the few aged cats, senile with boredom, still cared for in the park cages. They two made the expeditions that began, paragraph by paragraph, to grow in the city newssheets: Painter was the "big, burly man" who had stolen two legs of beef from a restaurant supplier while the supplier had been held at bay by a maddened dog, and who had then loped off into the blowing snow with the legs over his shoulders, about a hundred and a half pounds of meat and bone; if the supplier hadn't seen it done, he wouldn't have believed it.

If there had been more of a man's soul in either Sweets or Painter they would have seen the partnership they had entered on as astonishing, the adventures they had as tales at once thrilling and poignant; they would have remembered the face of the tall woman whom Painter gently divested of an enormous rabbit-fur coat, which he then wore always, the coat growing daily fouler. They would have dwelt on the moment when Painter, in the zoo, stood face to face with a lion, and looked at him, and the lion opened his lips to show teeth, uncertain why he was being looked at but recognizing a smell he knew he should respond to, and Painter's lip curled in a kind of echo of the lion's. They remembered none of this; or if they did, it was in a way that men would never be able to perceive. When much later Meric Landseer would try to tell Painter's story, he wouldn't be able to discover much about this part of it; Painter had already discarded most of it. He survived. That's what he could do; that was what he bent his skills to.

They did, though, come increasingly to understand each other. Painter knew he had to find a path that led safely out of the city; he knew it was impossible for him to live in the now-naked park for long without being seen, and taken. He didn't know that a full search hadn't been begun only because the old building where he had been prisoner, weakened by the blast, had fallen in on itself, and, since no one seemed capable of an official decision to dig it out, he had been assumed buried beneath a ton of moldered brick and wallpapered plaster. He knew that Sweets, like him, wanted to escape the park; Sweets knew the pack only lived here on men's sufferance and men's neglect, and would eventually be hunted down and shot or imprisoned or taken away in vans, if they didn't starve first. So it grew between them that when Painter left, the pack would follow him. Sweets laid down before Painter the burden of leadership, gratefully, and his heart with it. He had no idea what the freedom was that Painter promised, and didn't try to envision it. Once he had

taken the leo for master, all questions were for Sweets forever
answered.

It was really all he had ever wanted.

✻

The tunnel wasn't far north of the meat-packing houses the
pack had used to haunt in the early morning, snatching scraps
and suet from the discard bins, till the men armed with long
stinging batons came out to chase them away. Since the time one
of the pack had been cornered there by men and beaten and
stung to death by those sticks, they had avoided the places. But
Sweets remembered the tunnel. It was a dark, open mouth closed
with barricades; above it, orange lights went on and off in se-
quence. The city streets swept down to it from several directions
between stone bulwarks and then into its maw. Sweets had never
speculated about where it led or why, though once he had seen a
policeman mounted on a bike go in and not come out again.

By the time winter had grown old and filthy in the city,
Painter had settled on the tunnel, of all the exits Sweets and he
had investigated.

His and Sweets's breath rose whitely on the pale predawn air.
Painter looked down into the tunnel from the shelter of the bul-
wark's lip. A broken chain of dim yellow lights went away down
its center, but they lit nothing. Painter knew no more than
Sweets what was in there, but he supposed it led to the Northern
Autonomy; it was anyway the passage west, to the wild lands,
and that was all the freedom he needed, just now, to imagine.

Why were there no guards, as there were at the bridges?
Maybe there were, at the other end. Or maybe it was one of
those ancient duties that had come to be neglected, left up to
signs and fierce threats: DO NOT ENTER. NO THRU TRAFFIC.
VIOLATORS SUBJECT TO ARREST DETENTION RELOCATION. PRO-
VISIONAL REGIONAL GOVT. It's not in a leo's nature to speculate
about threats, dangers, punishment for ventures. He had tried to
work out what would happen once they were all inside, but
nothing came. So he only waited for the pack to gather.

They had come downtown through the night in their way, sep-
arately, yet never disattached from one another's odors and pres-

ence; they stopped to mark their way, stopped to investigate smells, food smells, rat smells, human smells. They circled downtown in a three-block quadrille. Sweets had stayed close to Painter in the vanguard, nervous over the direct, unhurried, unconcealed way he took but unwilling to be far from him. Now as the light grew he paced nervously, marked the place again, and kept his nose high for news of the others. In ones and twos and threes they assembled, all nervous at being so far from the smells of home as day broke; Duke especially was excited, his one proud ear swiveling for sounds.

Painter waited till he felt no further reluctance in Sweets to go (he'd never counted the pack or learned them all; only Sweets knew if they were all present) and then went down onto the tunnel approach, walking steadily through the yellow slush. The pack swarmed down behind him, staying close together now, not liking the tunnel but preferring its darkness to the exposed approach. Painter broke a place in the rotted wooden barricades; some of the pack had already slithered under, some clambered over. They were inside, moving quickly along the pale tiled wall. The clicking of the dogs' nails and the steady sound of Painter's boots were distinct, loud, instrusive in the silence.

The tunnel was longer than Painter had expected. It took wide, sinuous turns, as though they walked through the interior of a vast snake; the yellow lights glinted fitfully on the undersides of its scales. He thought they must be nearing the end when they had only passed the halfway mark, and he didn't know that at that mark—a dim white line at the river's center—their passage touched off a sensor connected to a police shack outside the far end of the tunnel.

Sweets ran on ahead, knowing he should around some turning see the daylight at the other end, wanting to be able to take Painter to it, to hurry him to it; but at the same time he wanted to be next to him. There was the pack also; impossible to keep them from lingering, from sounding when they passed through dark stretches where the light had failed. The best spur he could give them was to run on ahead and force them to follow; and it was when he had raced a distance ahead that he first heard the bike approaching them down the tunnel.

He stood stock still, fur standing, ears back. By the time the others had caught up with him the sound was loud. *No, keep on,* Painter said, and went on himself, drawing Sweets after him and the pack after Sweets. Now the noise was filling up the silence. Duke passed by Sweets, trembling, his face set, his odor loud and violent. The racket filled up every ear as they came to a turning; Sweets could hear nothing but it, and Painter's command to go on.

Around the turn the noise opened fanwise unbearably, and the black bike and its helmeted rider were bearing down on them. Whatever he had expected to find that had broken his sensor, it wasn't this; he had come up on them too fast; he backed off, braked, his engine broke into backfiring, and he skidded toward the animals. A black Doberman was flying through the air at him.

Duke, maddened by the noise, had attacked. He should have fled; he didn't know how. He only knew how to kill what attacked him. The noise attacked him and he leapt furiously to kill it. He struck with his mouth open as the bike twisted away like an animal in panic. Duke, the bike, and the man went down and spun in whipping circles sidewise violently into the wall. The noise was dead.

Go on, Painter said, beginning to run. *Run now, don't stop.* Sweets ran, blind fury behind his eyes; he didn't know how many of the others followed him, didn't care, didn't remember any longer where he ran, or why. He only knew that as he ran away a part of his being was left, caught, torn away, snared on the wreck of the bike and the broken body of Duke, brave Duke, mad Duke.

A half circle of light showed far off.

One after another, they pelted out of the tunnel, panicky; Heidi the poodle and Spike the wolfhound and Randy and the wild ones. All of them at last: leaping out, racing back within, running on away, and returning: all of them but Duke.

Painter came out, his broad chest heaving, the gun in his hand. His head snapped from side to side, looking for threats. There were none.

Sweets rushed to him, whimpering, lost now in sudden grief,

entangling himself in Painter's legs, wanting Painter to somehow absorb him, solve his pain and anger. *All but Duke,* he said. *All but Duke.* But Painter only shrieked once in impatience and kicked him from underfoot; then he started away down the empty avenue. *Get on,* he said. *Quick, away from here. Follow.* And Sweets knew that all he could do was follow, that this was all the answer he would ever have for any fear, any grief: *follow.* It would do.

They had gone on for some time before Sweets began to see the place that Painter had led them into.

Years before, during the wars, this band of city had been cleared, a buffer zone between the fractious island city and the Northern Autonomy. Even then, there had not been many people to evacuate; it had been for a long time a failure as a city. Now it was as deserted and hollowed as if it had been under the sea. The streets ran in the old rectangles around carious buildings, but the only human faces were those smilers, blinded with rust or torn and flapping, pictured in huge ads for products mostly no longer made.

Sweets could not have read, and Painter didn't see, the new signs that announced that the Northern Autonomy was now a Federal protectorate, occupied by Federal troops, requiring Federal passports. All they both knew, with increasing certainty, was that they hadn't escaped the city. It poured on past them as they walked, identical block after block. The sky had grown larger, the buildings lower; but it was still only dead city. When in the silence Painter began to hear, overhead, the quick insistent ticking, which seemed to have been pursuing him for years, he wasn't surprised. He didn't look up or run for cover, though Sweets pricked up his ears and looked up at Painter, ready at any moment to run, to hide. Painter walked on. The copter hovered, watching, and retreated.

From the copter the officer radioed in what he saw: a big man, maybe not a man, walking with some purpose through the streets, heading due north. "A lot of dogs around."

"Dogs, over?"

"Dogs. Lots of them. Over . . ."

Painter reached an impassable valley: the empty cut of a

sunken expressway. He turned northwest, walking along the edge of the expressway embankment. Far off as the road ran, but ahead, visible, the horizon could be seen, the true horizon, earth's, a bristle of leafless trees, soft rise of a brown hill, pale sun staining yellow a cape of winter clouds.

There, Painter said. *The freedom I promised you. Go now.*

Not without you.

Yes. Without me.

There were engines coming closer, coming through the maze of stone toward them. It must be toward them: they were the only living things here. The rest of the pack had fled along the intersecting streets. High above, the copter looked down, watching them run away, watching the big one in the fur coat and the dog who stayed beside him walk on. The copter could see where they would intersect with the cruisers: at the cut there, steep as a chute, that led down onto the expressway. He watched them come together.

The cruisers climbed the chute toward Painter and Sweets. They stopped, tires shrieking. Men popped out of them, shouting, armed. Painter stopped walking. *Go now,* he said. *Go where I told you.*

Sweets, torn in two, wanting only to die at Painter's side, yet overwhelmed by Painter's command to go, stood, riveted. The rest of the pack had fled. His mind, stretched almost to breaking, insisted that to follow his master now he must flee, must do what he could not. *Must.*

Painter started down the cut toward the waiting men. Why had he thought there was any escape from them, anywhere to run where they were not? He tossed away the gun, which clattered on the stone and spun for a moment like a top. He had never escaped; only, for a time, escaped notice.

Sweets watched Painter raise his arms gently as he walked toward the men. Then, before he could see them touch him, before they slew him with their touch, he turned and ran. He bounded north, fast, forcing his legs to stretch, to betray: *betray betray betray* his feet said as they struck the hard, endless stone of the city street.

SIX

Vox clamantis in deserto

On Mondays Loren came in to meet the packet plane that flew in once a week with supplies and mail to a small town ten miles or so from his cabin. To get into town, he had to canoe from his river-island observation station, where he spent most of the week, downriver to his cabin. From there he went on muleback to town. He rarely got back to the cabin before midnight; the next morning he would start out before dawn, and canoe back upriver to the island. Then, as though the whole of this journey had set him vibrating on a wrong note, he would have to spend most of that day untuning himself so that he could once again turn all his attention to the flock of Canada geese he had under observation. If he brought whiskey back from town to the cabin, he would struggle with himself to leave it in the cabin, having sometimes to go so far as to pour it out, or what was left of it. He kept himself from ever bringing any to the island; but this struggle made his first day's work at the island that much harder.

There weren't, every week, enough reasons for him to make the journey into town, as far as supplies or necessities went. Yet he made it. He tried hard to stock up on things, to deprive himself of logical reasons for the trip; yet when he couldn't stock up, when some supply was short that week in town and he saw that he would have no choice but to return, he felt a guilty relief. And even when he had utterly subjugated all these tricks, and had no reason to come in that even self-deception would buy, he came in anyway. Always. Because there was one thing he couldn't stock up on, and that was mail. Each week, that was new; each week it bore the same promise, and like the stupid chickens he had experimented with in school, each time there was no mail, he responded more fiercely the next time.

"No mail" meant no letter from Sten. He got enough other things. Dross. Newspapers he soon became unable to read with any understanding. Letters from other scientists he corresponded with about technical matters, about the geese. They weren't what brought him to town. Nor was it the whiskey either, really. There whiskey more or less resulted from the mail or the lack of it; or, what brought him into town for the mail brought him later to the whiskey. It all came to the same impulse. A syndrome, he knew he had to call it; yet it felt more like a small, circumscribed suburb of hell.

Even Loren Casaubon, who had dissected many animals, from a nematode worm to a macaque monkey—which began to decay loathsomely in the midst of his investigations, insufficiently pickled—even he located the seat of his fiercest and most imperative emotions in his heart. He knew better, but that's where he felt them. And it seemed, over the last months, that his heart had suffered physical strain from the vast charge of emotion it continuously carried: it felt great, heavy, painful.

That Monday the packet was late. Loren had a not-quite-necessary reshoeing done on the mule, watching the smith work gracelessly and hastily and wondering if these old skills that had once meant so much to the world, and seemed to be becoming just as necessary again, would ever be done as well as they once had been. He picked up a box of raisins and a dozen pencils. He went down to the muddy end of the street, to the rusting steel pier, and waited. He had been born patient, and his patience had undergone training and a careful fine-tuning in his work. He could remember, as a kid, waiting hours for a dormant snail to put out its head or a hunting fox to grow accustomed to his stationary, downwind presence and reveal himself. And he used those skills now to await, and not attempt to hasten, the guttural far-off sound, the clumsy bird.

It appeared from the wrong direction, made maneuvers around the skyey surface of the lake. Its ugly voice grew louder, and it settled itself down with a racing of engines and a speeding and slowing of props that reminded him of the careful wing-strategies of his landing geese. It must be, he thought, as its pontoons unsteadily gripped the water's stirred surface, the oldest plane in the world.

When the plane had been tied up, a single passenger got out. He hardly needed to stoop, so short he was. Leaning on a stick, he made his way down the gangway to the pier; sun and water-light glinted from his spectacles. When he saw Loren he came toward him in his odd, mincing gait. Loren noticed that he limped now as well; he made the process of walking look effortful and improbable.

"Mr. Casaubon." He removed the spectacles and pocketed them. "We've met. Briefly."

Loren nodded guardedly. His small, week-divided world was shaken by this creature's appearance. The beaten paths he had walked for months were about to be diverted. He felt unaccountably afraid. "What are you doing here?" He hadn't intended to sound hostile, but did; Reynard took no notice.

"In the first place, to deliver this." He took a travel-creased envelope from within his cape and held it toward Loren. Loren recognized, at once, the angular script; he had after all helped to shape it. Strange, he thought, how terrific is the effect of a fragment of him, outside myself, a genuine thing of his in the real world; how different than I imagine. This sense was the calm, self-observant eye of a storm of feeling. He took the letter from the strange, rufous fingers and put it away.

"And," Reynard said, "I'd like to talk to you. Is there a place?"

"You've seen Sten." The name caught in his throat and for a horrible moment he thought it might not come out. He had no idea how much the fox knew. He felt naked, as though even then telling all; as though his racing pulse were being taken.

"Oh yes, I've seen Sten," Reynard said. "I don't know what he's written you, but I know he wants to see you. He sent me to bring you."

Loren hadn't risen, not certain his legs would hold him; still, within, that calm eye observed, astonished at the power of a letter, a name, that name in another's mouth, to cause havoc in the very tissues and muscles of him.

"There's a bar up the street," he said. "The Yukon. Not the New Yukon. A back room. Go on up there. I'll be along."

He watched Reynard stick his way up the street. Then he turned away and sat looking out across the water as though he still waited for something.

*

After Gregorius had been murdered, the three of them—Sten, Mika, and Loren—began gradually to move into the big house. They took it over by degrees as Gregorius's spirit seemed to leave it; the kitchen first, where they ate, where the cook stuffed Sten and Mika out of pity for their orphanhood (though what Mika felt was not grief but only the removal of something, something that had been a permanent blockage at the periphery of vision, a hobble on the spirit; she had hardly known Gregorius, and liked him less). Next they moved into the living quarters, spreading out from their own nursery wing like advancing Mongols into the lusher apartments. The movement was noticed and disapproved of by the maids and housekeepers, for as long as they remained; but Nashe, utterly preoccupied with her own preservation and the prevention of anarchy, hardly noticed them at all. Now and then they would see her, hurrying from conference to conference, drawn with overwork; sometimes she stopped to speak.

The government was finally withdrawn altogether from the house and moved back to the capital. Nashe hadn't the personal magnetism to rule from seclusion, as Gregorius had done; and she didn't have Reynard for a go-between. She knew also that she had to dissociate herself from Gregorius; the memory of a martyr—even if most people weren't sure just what he had been martyred for, there were reasons enough to choose from—could only burden her. And Sten Gregorius must not figure in her story at all. At all. A small number of men in Blue continued to patrol the grounds; the children saw them now and again, looking bored and left over. The house belonged to the three of them.

Loren continued to be paid, and continued to teach, though he became less tutor than father, or brother—something else, anyway, inexorably. There had been a brief meeting with Nashe in which the children's future was discussed, but Nashe had not had her mind on it, and it ended inconclusively. Loren felt unaccountably relieved. Things would go on as they had.

There was a sense in which, of course, Sten at least was not an inheritor but a prisoner. He knew that, though he told no one what he knew. Except when this knowledge bore down on him, paralyzingly heavy, he was happy: the two people in the world he loved most, and who loved him unreservedly, were with him constantly. There were no rules to obey except his own, and Loren's, which came to the same thing. Sten knew that, with his father dead and Nashe departed, Loren drew all his power from the children's consent. But Loren's rules were the rules of a wise love, the only Sten had ever known, to be haggled over, protested sometimes, but never resented. He wondered sometimes, times when he felt at once most strong and most horribly alone, when it would happen that he would overthrow Loren. *Never!* his heart said, as loud as it could manage to.

Still there were lessons, and riding; less riding when winter began to close down fully and snow piled up in the stony pastures and ravines. Loren spent a long time trying to repair an ancient motor-sled left in a garage by the mansion's previous inhabitants.

"No go," he said at last. "I'll call somebody in the capital. They can't refuse you a couple of motor-sleds. . . ."

"No," Sten said. "Let's just snowshoe. And ski. We don't need them."

"They really more or less owe it to you."

"No. It's all right."

Later that month four new sleds arrived as a gift from a manufacturer; arrived with a hopeful photographer. Sten warily, ungraciously, accepted the sleds. The photographer was sent away, without Sten's picture, or his endorsement. The sleds were locked in the old garage.

Evenings they usually spent in the dim of the communications room, where deep armchairs deployed themselves around big screens and small monitors. They watched old films and tapes, listened to political harangues, watched the government and the religious channels. It didn't seem to matter. The droning flat persons were so far from them, so unreal, that it only increased their sense of each other. They could laugh together at the fat and the chinless and the odd who propounded to them the nature of things—Mika especially had no patience with rhetoric and a finely honed sense of the ridiculous—and the fat and the chinless and the odd, hugely enlarged or reduced to tininess by the screens, never knew they laughed. They could be extinguished by a touch on a lighted button. The whole world could be. It was a shadow. Only they three were real; especially when the heat failed in fuel shortages and they huddled together in a single thronelike chair, under a blanket.

Nashe was a fairly frequent shadow visitor in the communications room.

"Here's the straight pin," Mika said. Somehow this description of Mika's was hilariously apt, though none of them knew exactly why.

"She's got a hard job," Loren said. "The hardest."

"But look at that *nose*."

"Let's listen a minute," Sten said, serious. They all knew their fate was, however remotely, connected to this woman's. Sten felt it most. They must, sometimes, listen.

She was being asked a question about the Genesis Preserve. "Whatever crimes may have been committed within its borders are no concern of the Federal government," she said in her dry, tight voice. "Our long-standing agreements with the Mountain give us sole authority—at the Mountain's request—to enter it and deal with criminal activities. . . . No, we have had no such request. . . . No, it doesn't matter that it's a so-called Federal crime, if that phrase has any legal meaning anymore. I can only interpret all of this as an attempt by the Federal and the Union for Social Engineering to gain some quasi-legal foothold within this Autonomy. As Director, I cannot countenance that." She seemed to have to do that—announce her status—fairly frequently. "We know, I think, too much about USE to countenance any such activities." At least, Sten thought, she'll keep

USE out. She's got to fight them, take positions against them, because she benefited from their act, or what everybody thinks is their act. She can't make them illegal in the Autonomy, they're too strong for that. But she'll fight. Sten had inherited Loren's loathing of the intense men and women with their plastic briefcases and affectless voices.

"What happens," Sten asked, "if Nashe can't hold it together?"

"I don't know. Elections?"

Sten laughed, shortly.

"Well," Loren said. "Supposedly the Federal can intervene if there's severe civil disturbance. Whatever that means." His leg ached where Sten lay on it, but he wanted not to move. He wanted never to move. He put a careful left hand, as though only to accommodate his bigness between the two of them, in the hollow between Sten's neck and his hard shoulder. He waited for it to be thrown off, willing it to be thrown off, but it wasn't. He felt, within, another self-made rampart breached; he felt himself sink further into a realm, a darkness, he had only begun to see when the children and he inherited their kingdom: when it was too late to withdraw from its brink.

"What happens to us, then?" Mika said.

"They don't care abut us." Sten was quick, dismissive.

Yet later that night the old tape of him as a boy ran by again, on every screen; and the next night too. They watched it unroll. Not even Mika made fun of it. It seemed like a warning, or a summons.

There was an old-fashioned wooden sauna attached to what had been Gregorius's suite in the house. Here too, in the close, wood-odorous heat and dimness, they could hide together from whatever it was that seemed to press on them from the outside. When during the summer they had gone swimming together in the lakelets of the estate, Loren had been careful for their young shame; he'd worn a bathing suit, and so had they, until once on a humid night they'd gone without them and Mika had said that after all they'd only worn them for Loren's sake. After that they always went swimming naked, and later in the sauna too. They enjoyed the freedom of it, and they told each other that it was only sensible really; and forged without admitting it another bond between them.

"You start to feel," Sten said, "that you can't breathe, that the air's too hot to go in." He inhaled deeply.

"You're hyperventilating," Loren said. "You'll get dizzy."

Sten stood up, nearly fell, laughed. "I *am* dizzy. It feels weird."

Mika, feeling utterly molten within, as hot for once as she felt she deserved to be, rested her head against the wooden slatting. Drops of sweat started everywhere on her body and ran tickling along her skin. She watched Loren and Sten. Loren took Sten in a wrestler's hold around the middle and pressed; they were seeing how hyperventilated they could get, how giddy. Their wet feet slapped the floor. In the dim light their skin shone; they grappled and laughed like devils on a day off. At last they collapsed, gasping, weak. "No more, no more," Loren said.

Mika watched them. A man and a boy. She made comparisons. She seemed to be asleep.

"My father said," Sten gasped throatily, "that his father used to take a sauna, and afterward he ran out and rolled around in the snow. Naked."

"*Loco,*" Mika said.

"No," Loren said. "That's traditional."

"Wouldn't you catch cold?"

"You don't catch cold," Loren said, "from cold. You know that."

"You want to do it?" Sten said.

"Sure." Loren said it casually, as though he did it often.

"Not me," Mika said. "I'm just starting to get warm at last."

In fact they had to egg each other on for a while, but then they went bursting out into the suite, hallooing, through the French doors, and into the sparkling snow. Mika watched, hearing faintly through the glass their shouts—Loren's a deep roar, Sten's high and mad. She rubbed herself slowly with a thick towel. Loren wrestled Sten into a snowbank; she wondered if they were showing off for her. Loren was dark, thick, and woolly. Sten was lean, flaming pink now, and almost hairless; and shivering violently. Mika left the windows and went into the bedroom. She had already turned on her father's electric blanket; she always crawled beneath it after a sauna and slept. She glimpsed herself in one of the many tall mirrors, lean and brown and seeming not quite complete. She looked away, and slipped beneath the sheets.

She dreamed that she was married, in this bed, with her husband, whose features she couldn't make out; she felt an intense excitement, and realized that the mirrors in the room were her father's eyes, left there by him when he died just so he could witness this.

That winter was one of the hardest in living memory. Shortages made it harder: of fuel, of food, of everything. It didn't matter that Nashe and the few loyal ministers she had managed to keep around her blamed the Federal and USE for systematically blocking deliveries, causing delays at borders, issuing ambiguous safe-conducts or withholding them altogether: Nashe and the Directorate were whom the people blamed. There were mass demonstrations, riots. Blood froze on the dirty snow of city streets. USE journals and speakers, systematically and with charts and printouts, endlessly explained each crisis as a failure of human will and nerve, a failure to use human expertise, human reason—to make the world work. People listened. People marched for reason, rioted for reason. Along the borders of the Autonomy, troops—bands of armed men anyway, Federal men—kept watch, waiting. Candy's Mountain, self-sufficient and no hungrier this winter than another, felt, far-off, the pressure of envy.

Gregorius's house, too, felt far-off pressures. However they filled up the shortening days with activity, with hikes and study and snow castles, the days were haunted by the flickering hates and hungers they watched at night, as a day can be haunted by a bad dream you can't quite remember.

Every fine day that wasn't too bitterly cold, Hawk was set out on his high perch on the lawn. There was no way to fly him in this weather, so he had to be exercised on the lure, which Sten found tiresome and difficult. He went about it doggedly, but if Hawk was fractious or unaccommodating, it was a trial for both of them. Loren began to take over the duty, not letting Sten out

of it, but "helping" just to keep him company and keep him at it;
then gradually taking over himself.

"See," Loren said, "now he's roused, twice."

"Yes." Sten tucked his hands into his armpits. The day was
gray, dense with near clouds; wind was rising. It would snow
again soon. Hawk looked around himself at the world, at the humans, in quick, stern glances. His feathers filled out, his wings
and beak opened, he shook himself down: exactly the motion of
a man stretching.

"Three times." It was an old rule of falconry that a hawk that
has roused three times is ready to be flown: Loren's falconry was
a pragmatic blend of old rules, new techniques, life science, observation, and patience.

"Do you want to work him?"

"No."

The skills involved in flying a falcon at lure were in some
ways harder to acquire than hunting skills. A leather, sand-filled
bag on a long line, with the wings and tail of a bird Hawk had
slain last summer tied on realistically, and a piece of raw steak,
had to be switched from side to side, swung in arcs in front of
Hawk till he flew at it, and then twitched away before he could
bind to it. If Hawk bound to the lure, he would sit to eat, or try
to fly off with the lure, and the game would be over, with Hawk
the winner. If Loren swung the lure away too fast, giving him no
chance, Hawk would soon grow bored and angry. If Loren
should hit him with the heavy, flying lure, he'd be confused and
perhaps refuse to play—he might even be hurt.

Loren swung the lure before Hawk, tempting him, until
Hawk, his eyes flicking back and forth with the lure, threw
directly into the air and stooped to it, talons wide. Loren
snatched it away and swung it around his body like a man
throwing the hammer; Hawk swooped in a close arc around him,
seeking the lure. Loren watched Hawk's every quick movement,
playing with him, keeping him aloft, intent and careful and yet
reveling in his delicate control over this wild, imperious, self-
willed being. He swung, Hawk stooped; the lure flew in arcs
around Loren, and Hawk followed, inches from it, braking and
maneuvering, only a foot or two off the ground. Loren laughed

and cheered him, all his energies focused and at work. Hawk didn't laugh, only turned and curved with his long wings and reached out with his cruel feet to strike dead the elusive lure.

Sten watched for a time. Then he turned away and went back into the house.

When Loren, breathless and satisfied, came into the kitchen to get coffee, something hot, some reward, he found Sten with a cold cup in front of him, his chin in his hands.

"You don't, you know," Loren said, "have to best at everything. That's not required." As soon as he had said it, he regretted it bitterly. It was true, of course, but Loren had said it out of pride, out of success with Hawk, Sten's bird. He wanted to go to Sten and put an arm around him, show him he understood, that he hadn't meant what he said as crowing or triumph, just advice. And yet he had, too. And he knew that if he went to him, Sten would withdraw from him. That blond face, so whole and open and fine, could turn so black, so closed, so hateful. Loren made coffee, his exhilaration leaking away.

That night they turned away from the increasingly desperate government channels to watch "anything else," Mika said; "something not real—" something they could contain within the compass of their dream of three. But the channels were all full of hectoring faces, or were inexplicably blank. Then they turned on a sudden, silent image and were held.

The leo, with his ancient gun under his arm, stood at the flapping tent door. His great head was calm, neither inquisitive nor self-conscious; if he was aware his portrait was being taken he didn't show it. There was in his thick, roughly clothed body and blunt hands a huge repose, in his eyes a steady regard. Was it saintly or kingly he looked, or neither? The deep curl of his brow gave his eyes the easeful ferocity that the same curl gave to Hawk's eyes: pitiless, without cruelty or guile. He only stood unmoving. There was no sound but that peculiar electronic note of solitude and loneliness, the intermittent boom of wind in an unshielded microphone.

"Well," Mika said softly, "he's not real."

"Hush," Sten said. A mild boyish voice was speaking without haste:

"He was captured at the end of the summer by rangers of the Mountain and agents of the Federal government. Since that time he has not been heard of. The pride awaits word of him. They don't speculate about whether he was murdered, as he might well have been, in secret; whether he's imprisoned; whether he will ever return. For leos, there is no speculation, no fretting, no worry: it's not in their nature. They only wait."

Other images succeeded that lost king: the females around small fires, in billowing coats, their lamplike eyes infinitely expressive above their veiled mouths.

"God, look at their wrists," Mika said. "Like my legs."

The young played together, young blond ogres, unchildish, but with children's mad energy: cuffing and wrestling and biting with intent purpose, as though training for some desperate guerrilla combat. The females watched them without seeming to. Whenever a child came to a female, leaping onto her back or into her broad lap, he was suffered patiently; once they saw a female throw her great leg onto her child, pinning it down; the child wriggled happily, unable to free himself, while the female went on boiling something in a battered pot over the fire, moving with careful, wasteless gestures. No one spoke.

"Why don't they say anything?" Mika said.

"It's only humans who talk all the time," Loren said. "Just to hear talk. Maybe the leos don't need to. Maybe they didn't inherit that."

"They look cold."

"Do you mean cold, emotionless?"

"No. They look like they're *cold*."

And as though he knew that his watchers would have just then come to see that, the mild voice began again. "Like gypsies," he said, "like all nomads, the leos, instead of adapting their environment, adapt to it. In winter they go where it's warm. Far south now, other prides have already made winter quarters. For these, though, there will be no move this winter. The borders of this Autonomy are closed to them. They are, technically, all of them, fugitives and criminals. Somewhere in these mountains are Federal agents, searching for them; if they find them, they will be shot on sight. They aren't human. Due process need not be extended to them. They probably won't be found, but it hardly matters. If they can't move out of these snow-choked mountains, most of them will starve before game is again plentiful or huntable. This isn't strange; far from our eyes, millions of nonhumans starve every winter."

In half-darkness, the pride clustered around the embers of a fire and the weird orange glow of a cell heater. Some ate, with deliberate slowness, small pieces of something: dried flesh. In their great coats and plated muscle it was hard to see that any were starving. But there: held close in the arms of one huge female was a pale, desiccated child—no, it wasn't a child; she appeared a child within the leo's arms, but it was a human woman, still, dark-eyed: unfrightened, but seeming immensely vulnerable among these big beasts.

The image changed. A blond, beardless man, looking out at them, his chapped hands slowly rubbing each other. "We will starve with them," he said, his mild, uninflected voice unchanged in this enormous statement. "They are what is called 'hardy,' which only means they take a long time to die. They have strength; they may survive. We are humans, and not hardy. There's nothing we can do for them. Soon, I suppose, we'll only be a burden to them. I don't think they'll kill us, though I think it's within their right. When we're dead, we will certainly be eaten."

Again they saw the childlike girl within the leo's great protecting arms.

"We made these beasts," the voice said. "Out of our endless ingenuity and pride we created them. It's only a genetic accident that they are better than we are: stronger, simpler, wiser. Maybe that was so with the blue whale too, which we destroyed, and the gorilla. It doesn't matter; for when these beasts are gone, eliminated, like the whale, they won't be a reproach to our littleness and meanness any more."

The lost king appeared again, with his gun, the same image, the same awesome repose.

"Erase this tape," the voice said gently. "Destroy it. Destroy the evidence. I warn you."

The king remained.

When the tape had run out, the screen flickered emptily. The three humans huddled in their chair together before the meaningless static glow, and said nothing.

(Far off, in the cluttered offices of Genesis Section, Bree Landseer too sat silent, shocked, motionless before a screen; Emma Roth's large arm was around her, but Emma could say nothing, too full of the bitterest shame and most sinful horror she had ever felt. She, she alone, had brought this about; she had opened the doors to the hunters, the killers, the voracious—not the leos, no, but the gunmen in black coats, the spoilers, the Devil. She had delivered Meric and those beasts into the hands of the Devil. She couldn't weep; she only held Bree, unable to offer comfort, knowing that for this sin she could not now ever see the face of God.)

"It's not right," Sten said. "It's not fair. It's not even legal."

"Well," Loren said. "We don't really know the whole story. We didn't even see the whole tape."

Sten walked back and forth across the communications room. The screen's voiceless note had changed to an inscrutable hum, and dim letters said TRANSMISSION DISCONTINUED.

"We could help," Sten said.

"Help how?" Loren said.

"We could call Nashe. Tell her . . ."

"What? Those are Federal agents, he said."

"We could tell her we protest. We could tell everybody. The Fed. I'll call."

"No, you won't."

Sten turned to him, puzzled and angry. "What's wrong with you? Didn't you see them? They'll starve. They'll die."

"In the first place," Loren said, trying to sound reasonable but succeeding only in sounding cold, "we have no idea what the situation is. I've seen that man before. Haven't you? He's been on. He's from Candy's Mountain. He puts out propaganda, I've seen it, about how we should love the earth and how all animals are holy. Maybe this is just propaganda. How, anyway, did they get that tape out from wherever they are? Did you think of that?" In fact it had just occurred to Loren. "If they had the means to do that, don't they have the means to get food in, or get out themselves?"

Sten was silent, not looking at Loren. Beside him in the chair, Mika had drawn up into a ball, the blanket drawn up around her nose. He felt that she shrank from him.

"In the second place, there's nothing we can do. If there are Federal agents on the Preserve, presumably the Mountain let them in. It's their business. And anyway, what do the Feds want with the leos? What do you know about leos, besides what this guy said? Maybe he's wrong. Maybe the Feds are right."

Sten snorted with contempt. Loren knew how remote a chance there was that the Fed was acting disinterestedly. He knew, too, that Sten did have power—not, perhaps, with Nashe, but a vaguer power, a place in people's hearts: stronger maybe because vague. "In the third place . . ." In the third place, Loren felt a dread he couldn't, or chose not to, analyze at the thought of Sten's making himself known to the government, or to anyone; that seemed to make Sten horribly vulnerable. To what? Loren pushed aside the question. The three of them must hide quietly. It was safest. But he couldn't say that. "In the third place, I forbid it. Just take my word. It would lead to trouble if we got involved."

Mika squirmed out from under the blanket and stood hugging herself. Never, never would she learn to bear cold; it would remain always a deep insult, a grievous wrong. Watching the leos around their little fires, she had felt intensely the cold that bit them. "It's horrible."

"He's wrong, too, you know," Loren said softly, "about their being better than we are." The children said nothing, and Loren went on as though arguing against their silence. "It's like dog-lovers who say dogs are better than people, because they're more loyal, or because they can't lie. They do what they have to do. So do humans."

Sten got out of the chair and went to the control panel. He began to punch up channels, idly. Each channel yielded only blank static or a whining sign-off logo.

"I don't mean it's right that they should be starved or hunted,"

Loren said. Between the three of them a connection had been strained; the children had been deeply scandalized by what they had seen, and he must help them to think rightly about it. There was a proper perspective. "They have a right to life, I mean insofar as anything does. There are no bad guys, you know, not in life as a whole; it's understandable, isn't it, that people might hate and fear the leos, or be confused about them, and . . . Well. It's just difficult." He shut up. What he said wasn't reaching them, and he felt himself trying to draw it back even as he said it; it all sounded lame and wrong after their eyes had looked into the eyes of those beasts, and those crazy martyrs. Smug, wrong-headed martyrs: as wrong as the domineering men who hunted the leos, or the USE criminals who had exiled his hawks. Taking sides was the crime; and guilt and self-effacement, taking on this kind of crazy "responsibility"—that was only the opposite of heedless waste and man-centered greed.

"What's wrong?" Sten said. None of the channels was operating. He stopped nervously switching from one blankness to another, and without looking at Loren, left the room.

Mika still stood hugging herself. She had begun to shiver. "I thought they were monsters," she said. "Like the fox-man."

"They are," Loren said. "Just the same."

She turned on him, eyes fierce, lips tight. He knew he should mollify her, explain himself; but suddenly he too felt rigid and righteous: it was a hard lesson, about men and animals and monsters, life and death; let her figure it out.

Mika, turning on her heel and making her disgust with him obvious, left the room.

So it was only Loren, left sitting rageful and somehow ashamed in the electronic dimness, who saw the drawn face of Nashe appear very late on every channel. She was surrounded by men, some in uniform, all wearing the stolid, self-satisfied faces of bureaucratic victors. Her voice was an exhausted whisper. Her hands shook as she turned the pages of her announcement, and she stumbled over the sentences that had been written for her. She told the Autonomy that its government was hereby dissolved; that because of serious and spreading violence, instability and disorder, the Federal government had been obliged to enter the Autonomy in force to keep the peace. The Autonomy was now a Federal protectorate. Eyes lowered, she said that she had been relieved of all powers and duties; she urged all citizens to obey the caretaker government. She folded her paper then, and thanked them. For what? Loren wondered.

When she was done, fully humiliated, she was led away from the podium and off-screen, with two men at her side, as nearly a prisoner as any thief in custody. A thick-faced man Loren remembered as having been prominent on the screens recently—one of those they had laughed at and extinguished—spoke then, and gave the venerable litany of the coup d'état: a new order of peace and safety, public order was being maintained, citizens were to stay in their homes; all those violating a sundown curfew would be arrested, looters shot, the rest of it.

They played the old national anthem then, a scratchy, dim recording as though it were playing to them out of the far past, and the new government stood erect and listened like upright sinners to a sermon. An old film of the Federal flag was shown, the brave banner waving in some long-ago wind. It continued to wave, the only further message there would be that night from the masters, as though they were saying, like a wolf pack, Here is our mark; it is all we need to say; this place is ours, you have been warned, defy it if you dare.

The waves that the packet plane had made in its landing continued to rebound from around the lake shore and slosh gently against the pilings in arcs of coming and going.

Loren saw that the letter began with his own name, but then he rushed along the close-packed lines so fearfully and voraciously that he understood nothing of the rest of it, and had to return, calm himself, and attend to its voice. "I hope you are doing all right where you are. I couldn't get any news for a long time and I wondered what had happened with you." Wondered how, how often, when, with what feelings? "I've heard about what you're doing, and it sounds very interesting, I wish we could talk about it. This is really very hard to write." Loren felt like a stab the pause that must have fallen before Sten wrote

that sentence; and then felt well up from the stab a flood of love
and pity so that for a moment the words he looked at glittered
and swam illegibly. "For a lot of reasons I can't tell you exactly
where we are now, but I wanted you to know that I'm all right
and Mika is too. I know that's not much to say after so long, but
when you're an outlaw and a murderer (that's what I'm called
now) you don't write much down.

"I think a lot about what happened and about the fun we had
alone in the house and how we were happy together. I wish it
hadn't ended. But I did what I thought I had to, and I guess so
did you. It's funny, but even though it was me who left, when I
think about it it seems like it was you who ran out on me! Anyway I hope we can be friends again. As you will find out, I need
all the friends I can get. I need your help. You always helped
me, and whatever good I am, I owe to you. I've changed a lot."
It was signed "Your good friend Sten."

Beneath his signature he had added another sentence, less like
an afterthought than an admission that he had known all along
he must make but which had been wrung from him only at the
last moment: "I'm very very sorry about Hawk."

✳

For a tense and ominous week after Nashe's fall the three of
them waited for the new government to notice them. It would be
like the Federal in its mindless thoroughness to attempt something against the heir of Gregorius, but nothing happened.
They remained as free within the estate as they had been. People
came, not sent by any government, but impelled by some need to
gather at a center. They camped outside the walls or loitered in
groups beyond the barred gates, looking in. They went away,
others came. Still no official change in their status came.

But Sten felt a change. Where before he had felt isolated, hidden, protected even in his redoubt with Loren and Mika, safe
from the consequences of his complicity in his father's murder,
now he began to feel imprisoned. The night when he had
watched the leos, cut off and surrounded in their mountains, and
listened to the pale powerless man admit that he and the girl
would die with them, unable to struggle against it, Sten had felt

torn between contempt and longing: he wanted somehow to help them; he knew he would never, never surrender like that, accede to powerlessness as that man had; and at the same time he saw that he too was as chained, as powerless as they were.

Now Nashe had given in, and the same Federal government that hunted the leos surrounded Sten, strangling him, waiting for him to starve to death. He felt a suffocating sense of urgency, a feeling that wouldn't diminish; the more the invisible chains bound him, the harder he pressed against them.

Even Loren, now, seemed interested only in restraining him. Where before they had stood in a kind of balance, each, as it were, holding a hand of Mika's to keep themselves stable, now they had begun to rock dangerously. Loren issued commands; Sten flouted them. Loren lectured; Sten was mum. Sten saw, shocked, that Loren was afraid; and not wanting to, he began to press Loren's fear, as though to see if it was really real.

"Are they still out there?" Mika asked.

"Don't acknowledge them," Loren said. "Don't encourage them. Don't . . ."

Sten turned away from the bulletproof window of his father's office, where he had been spying with binoculars at two or three silent, overcoated people who could be seen beyond the gate. "Why is it," he said to Loren coldly—it was his father's penetrating tone—"that you're always hovering over me?"

Loren, knowing he couldn't say "Because I love you," said, "Don't do anything dumb. It's all I meant," and left.

When he was gone, Sten took out the letter again. It had been given to him by the man who brought provisions to the house, handed to him without a word as the man left the kitchen. It wasn't addressed. It was carelessly typed: *If after the manner of men, I have struggled with beasts at Ephesus, what advantageth it me, if the dead rise not?* Beneath this, which Mika thought was a quote from the Bible, was a series of numbers and letters. Sten figured out, after much study, that these were geographical co-ordinates, elevations, compass directions. Perhaps he wouldn't have given it that much study, except that carefully, childishly, scrawled at the bottom was a single letter for a signature: *R.*

"We should ask Loren," Mika said.

Sten only shook his head. Why should Reynard reveal to him the place where the leos were hiding? Because Sten was sure now that this was what it was. The maps kept in his father's office showed him the place Reynard had directed him to: a place in the mountains that bordered the Autonomy on the north, the crest of Genesis Preserve.

"Could it be," Mika said, "that he meant we should help them? Get to them somehow, and help?"

When, in the old schoolhouse, Reynard had given him this house and this safety, even, probably, his life, in exchange for silence, he had told him: be neither predator nor prey. If that was so, he was in growing trouble here, because he was fleeing, like prey, hiding: from the government, from the people out there— from Loren. If now Reynard had directed him to rise, as from the dead, was it for the leos he was to do so? And did he dare anyway? He did, desperately, want Loren's advice and help. But Loren had made himself clear about the leos.

"Would you dare?" he said to Mika. "Would you dare go up into the mountains, bring them food?"

Her black eyes grew round at the thought. "What will we tell Loren?"

"Nothing." Sten felt flooded with a sudden resolve. This would be the unbinding he had been waiting for: he had been called on, and he chose to answer. With Mika, if she dared; alone, if that was how it had to be.

Mika watched him fold the letter carefully, once, again, again, as though he were laying away a secret resolve. Without looking at her, he told her the story of how their father had been killed, and what he had done, and why they had been safe in the house.

"You could stay," he said. "You'd be safe, here, with Loren."

She sat silent a long time. It had begun to snow again, a sleety, quick-falling snow that could be heard striking, like a breath endlessly drawn. She thought of them naked, laughing in snow.

"We could use sleds," she said at last.

That week the telephone lines into the house were cut— perhaps by the snow, perhaps deliberately, they were given no explanation—and Loren began making weekly trips to the nearest town, nearly five miles off, to call their suppliers and to buy newspapers, to see if he could perceive some change in their status, guess what was to become of them. There was no one he trusted whom he could call, no old government official or family lawyer. He knew it was madness to try to hide this way; it couldn't last. But when he contemplated bringing Sten to official attention, to try to get some judgment made, he shrank from it. Whatever came of it, he was certain they would somehow take him away, somehow part them. He couldn't imagine any other conclusion.

Returning from town, he pushed his way through the small knot of people at the front gate and let himself in at the wicket. When questions were asked he only smiled and shrugged as though he were idiotic, and concentrated on passing quickly through the wicket and getting it locked again, so as not to tempt anyone to follow, and went quickly up the snow-choked road, away from their voices.

He stopped at the farmhouse and went in. A small cell heater had been brought down from the house and was kept going here always, though it barely took the chill from the stone rooms. That was all Hawk needed.

Hawk was deep in molt. He stood on his screen perch, looking scruffy and unhappy. Two primaries had fallen since Loren had last looked in on him—they fell always in pairs, one from each side, so that Hawk wouldn't be unbalanced in flight—and Loren picked them up and put them with the others. They could be used to make repairs, if ever Hawk broke a feather; but chiefly they were saved as a baby's outgrown shoes are saved.

The day was calm and bright, the sun almost hot. He'd take Hawk up to the perch on the lawn.

Speaking softly to him, with a single practiced motion he slipped the hood over Hawk's face and pulled it tight—it was too stiff, it needed oiling, there was no end to this falconer's job —and then pulled on his glove. He placed the gloved hand beneath Hawk's train and brushed the back of his legs gently. Hawk, sensing the higher perch behind him, instinctively stepped backward, up onto the glove. He bated slightly as Loren moved his hand to take the leash, and only when Hawk was firmly settled on his wrist did Loren untie the leash that held him to the perch. As between thieves, there was honor between falconer and bird only when everything was checked and no possibility for betrayal—escape—was allowed.

He walked him in the house for a time, stroking up the feathers on his throat with his right forefinger till Hawk seemed content, and then went out into the day, blinking against the glare from the snow, and up to the perch on the wide lawn. From behind the house, he thought he heard the faint whistle of the new motor-sleds being started. He tied Hawk's leash firmly to the perch with a falconer's one-handed knot, and brushed the perch against the back of his legs so that Hawk would step from his hand up to the perch. He unhooded him. Hawk roused and opened his beak; the inner membranes slid across his dazzled eyes. He looked with a quick motion across the lawn to where three motor-sleds in quiet procession were moving beyond a naked hedge.

"What's up?" Loren shouted, pulling off his glove and hurrying toward them. Mika, and Sten, to whose sled the third, piled up with gear wrapped in plastic, was attached, didn't turn or stop. Loren felt a sudden, heart-sickening fear. "Wait!" Damn them, they must hear. . . . He broke through the hedge just as the sleds turned into the snowy fields that stretched north for miles beyond the house. Loren, plowing through the beaten snow, caught Sten's sled before Sten could maneuver his trailer into position to gather speed. He took Sten's arm.

"Where are you going?"

"Leave me alone. We're just going."

Mika had stopped her sled, and looked back now, reserved, proud.

"I said *where?* And what's all this stuff?"

"Food."

"There's enough here for weeks! What the hell . . ."

"It's not for us."

"Who, then?"

"The leos." Sten looked away. He wore snow glasses with only a slit to look through; it made him look alien and cruel. "We're bringing it to the leos. We didn't tell you because you'd only have said no."

"Damn right I would! Are you crazy? You don't even know where they are!"

"I do."

"How?"

"I can't tell you."

"And when will you come back?"

"We won't."

"Get out of that sled, Sten." They had meant to sneak away, without speaking to him, without asking for help. "I said get out."

Sten pulled away from him and began to pull at the sled's stalled engine. Loren, maddened by this betrayal, pulled him bodily out of the sled and threw him away from it so that he stumbled in the snow. "Now listen to me. You're not going anywhere. You'll get this food back where it belongs"—he came up behind Sten and pushed him again—"and get those sleds out of sight before . . . before . . ."

Sten staggered upright in the snow. His glasses had fallen off, but his face was still masked, with something cold and hateful Loren had never seen in it before. It silenced him.

Mika had left her sled and came toward them where they stood facing each other. She looked at Loren, at Sten. Then she came and took Sten's arm.

"All right," Loren said. "All right. Listen. Even if you know where you're going. It's against the law." They made no response. "They're hunted criminals. You will be too."

"I am already," Sten said.

"What's that supposed to mean?"

"You wouldn't have helped, would you?" Mika said. "Even if we'd told you."

"I would have told you what I thought."

"You wouldn't have helped," she said with quiet, bitter contempt.

"No." Even as he said it, Loren knew he had indicted himself before them, hopelessly, completely. "You just don't throw everything up like this. What about the animals? What about

Hawk?" He pointed to the bird on his perch, who glanced at them when they moved, then away again.

"You take care of him," Sten said.

"He's not my hawk. You don't leave your hawk to someone else. I've told you that."

"All right." Sten turned and strode through the snow to the perch. Before Loren could see what he was doing, he had drawn a pocketknife and opened it; it glinted in the snowlight.

"No!"

Sten cut Hawk's jesses at the leash. Loren ran toward them, stumbling in the snow.

"You little *shit!*"

Hawk for a moment didn't notice any change, but he disliked all this sudden motion and shouting. He was in a mood to bate —to fly off his perch—though he had learned in a thousand bates that he would only fall, flapping helplessly head downward. Sten had taken off his jacket, and with a sudden shout waved it in Hawk's face. Hawk, with an angry scream, flew upward, stalled, and found himself free; for a moment he thought to return to the perch, but Sten shouted and waved the jacket again, and Hawk rose up in anger and disgust. It felt odd to be free, but it was a good day to fly. He flew.

"Now," Sten said when Loren reached him, "now he's nobody's hawk."

With an immense effort, Loren stemmed a tide of awful despair that was rising in him. "Now," he said, calmly, though his voice shook, "go down to the farm and get the long pole and the net. With the sleds, we might be able to get him after dark. He's gone east to those trees. Sten."

Sten pulled on his jacket and walked past Loren back to the sleds.

"Mika," Loren said.

She stood a moment between them, hugging herself. Then, without looking back to Loren, she went to her sled too.

Loren knew he should go after them. Anything could happen to them. But he only stood and watched them struggle with the sleds, get them aligned and started. Sten gave Mika a quiet command and put his snow glasses on again. He looked back once to

Loren, masked, his hands on the sticks of the sled. Then the sleds moved away with a high whisper, dark and purposeful against the snow.

＊

"Yes," Reynard said. "It was I who told Sten where the leos were. It was very clever of him to have worked it out."

"And you had brought out the film, too, that we saw?"

"Yes."

"How did you get to them, find them, without being stopped? And back again?"

Reynard said nothing, only sat opposite Loren at the water-ringed table.

"You made Sten a criminal. Why?"

"I couldn't let the leos die," Reynard said. "You can understand my feelings."

Actually that was impossible. His thin, inexpressive voice could mean what it said, or the opposite, or nothing at all. His feelings were undiscoverable. Loren watched him scratch his whiskery chops with delicate dark fingers; it made a dry-grass sound. Reynard took a black cigarette from a case and lit it. Loren watched, trying to discover, in this peculiarly human gesture of lighting tobacco, inhaling smoke, and expelling it, what in Reynard was human, what not. It couldn't be done. Nothing about the way Reynard used his cigarette was human, yet it was as practiced, casual, natural—as appropriate—as it would be in a man.

"He saved them," Reynard said, "from death. Not only the leos, but two humans as well. Don't you think it was brave of him? The rest of the world does."

From his papers, reaching him usually a week late, Loren had learned of Sten's growing fame; it was apparent even here, far north of the Autonomy. "It was very foolhardy," was all he said.

"He took risks. There was danger. Unnecessary, maybe. Maybe if you'd been there, to help . . . Anyway, he brought it off."

Loren drank. The whiskey seemed to burn his insides, as though they had already been flayed open by his feelings. He couldn't tell the fox that he hated him because the fox had taken Sten from him. It wasn't admissible. It wasn't even true. Sten had gone on his own to do a difficult thing, and had done it. Mika, who loved him, had gone with him. Loren had been afraid, and so he had lost Sten. Was that so, was that the account he must come to believe?

"He had you, didn't he?" Loren said.

"Well. I'm not much good now. I was never—strong, really, and you see I'm lamed now."

"You seem to get around."

"I'm also," Reynard said as though not hearing this, "getting very old. I'm nearly thirty. I never expected a life-span that long. I feel ancient." Smoke curled from his nostrils. "There is a hunt on for me, Mr. Casaubon. There has been for a long time. I've thrown off the scent more than once, but it's growing late for me. I'm going to earth." He smiled—perhaps it was a smile—at this, and the ignored ash of his cigarette fell onto the table. "Sten will need you."

"What is it you wanted from Sten?" Loren asked coldly. He tried to fix Reynard's eyes, but like an animal's they wouldn't hold a stare. "Why did you choose him? What for?"

Reynard put out the cigarette with delicate thoroughness, not appearing to feel challenged. "Did you know," Reynard said, "how much Sten means in the Northern Autonomy? And outside it too?" He moved slowly in his chair; he seemed to be in some pain. "There is a movement—one of the kind that men seem so easily to work up—to make Sten a kind of king."

"King?"

"He'd make a good one, don't you think?" His long face split again in a smile, and closed again. "That he's an outlaw now, and hunted by the Federal, is only appropriate for a young king —a pretender. The Federal has mismanaged their chance in the Autonomy, as it had to. Sten seems to people everywhere to be —an alternative. Somehow. Some kingly how. Strong, and young, and brave—well. If there are kings—kings born—he's one. Don't you agree?"

From the time Loren had opened the *North Star* magazine he had been a subject of Sten's; he knew that. That Sten must one day pick up a heritage that lay all around him he had always known too, though he had tried to ignore it. He felt, momentarily, like Merlin, who had trained up the boy Arthur in secrecy; saw that what he had trained Sten to be was, in fact, king. There wasn't any other job he was suited for.

"It's a fact about kings," Reynard said, "that they must have around them a certain kind of person. Persons who love the king in the king, but know the man in the king. Persons for whom the king will always be king. Always. No matter what. I don't mean toadies, or courtiers. I mean—subjects. True subjects. Without them there are no kings. Of course."

"And you? Are you a king's man?"

"I'm not a man."

Already the northern afternoon was gathering in the light. Loren tried to count out the feelings contending in him, but gave it up. "Where is he now?"

"Between places. Nowhere long." He leaned forward. His voice had grown small and exhausted. "This is a difficulty. He needs a place, a place absolutely secret, a base. Somewhere his adherents could collect. Somewhere to hide—but not a rathole." Again, the long, yellow-toothed smile. "After all, it will be part of a legend someday."

Loren felt poised on the edge of a high place, knowing that swarming up within him were emotions that would eventually make him step over. He drank quickly and slid the empty glass away from him on a spill of liquor. "I know a place," he said. "I think I know a place."

Reynard regarded him, unblinking, without much interest, it seemed, as Loren described the shot tower, where it was, how it could be gotten to; he supposed the food, the cans anyway, and the cell heater would still be there.

"When can you be there?" Reynard said when he had finished.

"Me?" Reynard waited for an answer. "Listen. I'll help Sten, because he's Sten, because . . . I owe it to him. I'll hide him if I can, keep him from harm. But this other stuff." He looked away from Reynard's eyes. "I'm a scientist. I've got a project in hand here." He drew in spilled liquor on the table—no, not that name, he rubbed it away. "I'm not political."

"No." Reynard, unexpectedly, yawned. It was a quick, wide motion like a silent bark; a string of saliva ran from dark palate to long, deep-cloven tongue. "No. No one is, really." He rose, leaning on his stick, and walked up and down the small, smelly barroom—deserted at this hour—as though taking exercise. "Geese, isn't it? Your project." He stopped, leaning heavily on the stick, holding his damaged foot off the ground and turning it tentatively. "Isn't there a game, fox and geese?"

"Yes."

"A grid, or paths . . ."

"The geese try to run past the fox. He catches them where paths join. Each goose he catches has to help him catch others."

"Ah. I'm a—collector of that kind of lore. Naturally."

"My geese," Loren said, "are prey for foxes."

"Yes?"

"And they know it. They teach it—the old ones teach the young. It doesn't seem to be imprinted—untaught goslings wouldn't run from a fox instinctively. The older ones teach them what a fox looks like, by attacking foxes, in a body, and driving them off. The young ones learn to join in. I've seen my flock follow a fox for nearly a mile, honking, threatening. The fox looked very uncomfortable."

"I'll leave you now," Reynard said. If he had heard Loren's story he didn't express it. "The plane will be going. There are still a few things I have to do." He went to the door.

"No rest for the wicked," Loren said.

Reynard had been walking out of the bar without farewell. He turned at the door. "Teach your goslings," he said. "Only be sure you know who is the fox."

When he had gone out into the pall of the afternoon—tiny, old, impossible—Loren went to wake the bartender and have his glass filled again. The letter where it lay in his breast pocket seemed to press painfully against his heart.

✳

Nothing is more soothing to a scientist than the duplication of another scientist's results. When Loren had left the empty brown mansion he had thought only of a place to lose himself, a far, unpeopled place to hide; but he knew he would have to occupy himself as well, engage all his faculties in a difficult task, if he was to escape—even momentarily—the awful rain he seemed always to be standing in when he thought of Sten and Mika.

They meant what they had said: they didn't come back. He had known they wouldn't. After ten days had passed, and a new fall of snow had covered their traces, he called the Autonomy police and reported them suddenly missing. The police forces were in the process of being reorganized, and after some lengthy interrogations, in which he communicated as little as he could without arousing suspicion, the matter seemed to be dropped, or filed, or forgotten amid larger bureaucratic struggles. He thought once during a police interview (Federal this time) that he was about to be beaten into a confession, a confession of something; he almost wished for it: there was no one else to punish him for what he had done.

What had he done?

He drew his almost-untouched government salary, got a small, reluctant grant from Dr. Small, and went north out of the Autonomy to the breeding grounds of the Canada geese. One of the great ethologists of the last century had made extensive observations of the European greylag goose; his records were famous, and so were his conclusions, about men and animals, instinct, aggression, bonding. He had extended his conclusions to all species of the genus *Anser,* the true goose. The Canada goose isn't *Anser* but *Branta.* It would take months—healing, annealing months alone—to compare the century-old observations of *Anser* behavior with that of *Branta.* The resulting paper would be a small monument, a kind of extrusion out of misery, like an oyster's pearl.

Reading again the old man's stories—for that's what they seemed to be, despite their scientific apparatus, stories of love and death, grief and joy—what Loren felt was not the shocking sense its first readers had, that men are nothing more than beasts, their vaunted freedoms and ideals an illusion—the old, old reaction of men who had first read Darwin—but the opposite. What the stories seemed to say was that beasts are not less than men: less ingenious in expression, less complex in possibility, but as complete; as feeling; as capable of overmastering sorrow, hurt, rage, love.

The center of greylag life is the triumph ceremony, a startlingly beautiful enchainment of ritualized fighting redirected aggression, a thousand interlocking, self-generating calls and responses. The geese perform this ceremony in pairs, bonded for life; bonded by the dance. The old man had said: the dance does not express their love; the dance *is* their love. When one of a pair is lost—caught in electric wires, shot, trapped—the other will search ceaselessly for it, calling in the voice a lost gosling calls its mother. Sometimes, after much time, they will bond again, begin again; sometimes never.

Mostly the pairs are male-female, but often they are male-male; in this case there is sometimes a satellite female, lover of one of the males, who will be satisfied to share their love, and can intrude herself sufficiently into their triumphs to be mounted and impregnated. This isn't the only oddity of their bonding: there are whole novels among them of attempted bondings, flawed affairs, losses, rivalries, heartbreaks.

Loren had seen much of this among his geese, though their social life seemed frozen at an earlier, less complex state; their ceremonies were less expressive; their emotions, therefore—from the observer's point of view—were less extensive. He had carefully noted and analyzed ritual behavior, knew his flock well, and had seen them court, raise young, meet threats, in a kind of stable, unexciting village life. Whether beneath the squabbles and satisfactions of daily life a richer current ran—as it does in every village—didn't interest him as a scientist. Unexpressed needs and feelings were either unfelt or unformed; they couldn't be analyzed.

Yet he wanted them to tell him more. Was *Anser* more human than *Branta*, or had the old man's stories been only parables in the end, like Aesop's?

He had told of two males, both at the top of the flock hierarchy, who had bonded, who danced only for each other. The proudest, the strongest, they had no rivals, no outsiders from whom to protect each other; few came near them. Their ceremony—change and change again—became more and more

intense; they did it for hours. At last the weight of emotion that
the ceremony carried became too great; the aggression that it
modeled and ritualized became too intense, having no other out-
let. The ritual broke into real, unmediated aggression; the birds
bit and beat at each other with strong wings, inflicting real
wounds.

The bond was broken. Immediately after, the two birds parted
—went to opposite sides of the pond, avoided each other. Never
performed for each other again. Once, when by error they encountered each other face to face in the middle of the pond,
each immediately turned away, grooming excitedly, bill-shaking,
in a state the old man said could only be described as intense
embarrassment.

"Could only be described," Loren said aloud to the frosty
night, "as intense embarrassment." The mule jogged, Loren
swayed drunkenly. *"Intense. Embarrassment."*

How could he see Sten again? If they met, wouldn't there be
between them an embarrassment that would make any communication impossible? Seeing him again, having him before his
eyes again, had been Loren's obsession for months; but now that
he had been invited to it, for real, he could only imagine that he
would be full of shame and hurt and embarrassment. Better to
let the enormous engine of his love, disengaged from its object,
grind and spin on uselessly within him him till it finally ran out
of fuel or fell to pieces, to silence.

Yet Sten had sent for him. He groaned aloud at the stars. Far
down within him he seemed to see—whiskey, only whiskey, he
told himself—a possibility he had long discounted, a possibility
for happiness after pain.

The next morning, to cleanse himself of shame and hope and
the sour humors of the whiskey, he plunged naked up to his neck
in the icy river, shouting, trying to shout out all the impurity he
felt within; he splashed his face, rubbed his neck, waded onto
the shore, and stood shivering fiercely. By an act of will he
ceased shivering. There wasn't any weakness, any impatience,
any badness in him that he couldn't, by a similar act of will,
overcome.

Quieter then, he dressed, slipped the canoe, and started

upriver. The river was low and slow; leaves floated on it, fell continuously on it, clogged its tributaries. Dense clouds were pillowed at the horizon, and overhead a high, fast wind, so high it couldn't be felt below, marked the October blue with chalk marks of cloud. Summer was long over here. Last night's frost had been hard.

During that week, his geese were restless, rising up in a body, circling for a time, realighting excited and nervous. It was as though his peaceful village had been swept by a bizarre religious mania. Old quarrels were forgotten. Nest sites were left unguarded. They were aligning themselves, making a flying force. The time had come for their migration. On Monday—the day that he would have gone into town—he awoke before dawn, and had barely time to dress before he saw that this would be the day of their leaving.

Loren had identified the commodore and his lieutenants (they were called that in his notes, though they would not be in his final paper) and noted their strategy meetings and route conferences. Now in the dawn the hair stood on Loren's neck: was it because, over the months, he had become almost one of them that he knew with such certainty that this was the day—had it been communicated to him as it had been to each of them, did his certainty add to the growing mass of their certainty, inciting them to fly?

All that morning he photographed and noted, ill almost with excitement, as they knitted their impulses together. Again and again small groups pounded into the air, circled, alighted, reascended. About noon the commodore and some of the ranking members of his staff, male and female, arose, honking, and sailed off purposefully, making a tentative, ragged V: maneuvers. They didn't return; with his glasses, Loren scanned from the crook of a tall tree, and saw them waiting in a watermeadow somewhat northeast. The rest still honked and argued, getting up nerve. Then the commodore and his staff flew back, sailing low and compellingly over the flock, going due south; and in a body the others were drawn after them, rising in a multiple fan of black and brown wings, attaching themselves.

For as long as he could, Loren followed them with the glasses, watched their V form neatly against the hard blue sky marked with wind. They were wind. They were gone.

Alone again, Loren sat in the crook of the tree. Their wings' thunder and their cries had left a new void of silence. Winter seemed suddenly palpable, as though it walked the land, breathing coldly. He remembered winter.

After Sten and Mika had gone out of sight, he had spent that day searching for Hawk on snowshoes, with lure and net and pole; walked himself to exhaustion through the woods, purposelessly, having no idea where Hawk might go and seeing no trace of him. If he had found a dead bird, if he had seen blood on the snow, he would have gone on, not eating, not sleeping; but he saw nothing. Night was full when he came back to the empty house, amost unable to stand; the pain, though, had been driven almost wholly to his legs and feet, where he could bear it.

Once inside, however, in the warm, lamplit emptiness, it took him again head to toe. He dropped the useless hawking gear. He would find, capture, hold, nothing, no one. He climbed the stairs, almost unable to bend his knees, and went to Sten's room. He didn't turn on the light. He smelled the place, the discarded clothing, the polished leather, the books, Sten. He felt his way to the narrow bed and lay down, pressing his face into the pillow, and wept.

All the wild things fly away from me, he thought now, in the crook of the tree by the empty river. Every wild thing that I love. If they don't know how to fly, I teach them.

Wiping the cold tears from his beard, he climbed down from the tree and stood in the suddenly pointless encampment. Stove, tent, supplies, canoe. Shirt drying on a branch. Camera, recorder, notebooks. He had tried to make a home in the heart of the wild, to be quiet there and hear its voice. But there was no home for him there.

Methodically, patiently, he broke camp. Like the geese, but far more slowly, he would go south. Unlike them, he was free not to; and yet knew there was nothing else he could do.

SEVEN

In at the death

The last truck left Caddie off at an interchange a mile or more from the center of the city. The driver pointed out to her the slim white needle, impossibly tall, just visible beyond the river, and said this was as close as he came to it; so she swung down from the cab and began to walk toward it.

It had been terrifying at first to stand alone beside the vast spread of naked highway, waiting for the trucks. For a year she had rarely been out of the company of the pride, had forgotten, if she'd ever known, how to discount the terror of this inhuman landscape, stone and sounds and vast signs and speed. She wanted to run from it, but there was no one who could do this but she; certainly none of the leos, and Meric was known from the tape in which she had appeared only briefly. So she had stood waiting in a thin rain for the trucks—there was almost no other traffic—holding out her thumb in the venerable gesture. She recoiled when they bore down on her and barreled past, wrapped in thin veils of mist that their tires pressed out from the road's wet surface; but she stayed.

When at last one, with a long declension of gears, slowed and stopped fifty yards down from where she stood, her heart beat fast as she ran to it. She felt for the gun in her belt, under her jacket; she felt her breasts move as she ran.

They were only truck drivers, though, she came quickly to learn, the same she had dealt with every week in Hutt's bar.

They talked a lot, but that didn't bother her. Only once did she feel compelled to mention the gun, casually, in passing: a person has to protect herself.

In a way, it was the small talk that was harder to answer: Where are you from? Why are you going to Washington? Who are you?

Looking for a relative. Promise of a job. Come from, well, north. Up there. Because she couldn't tell them that she had come hundreds of miles at the direction of the fox to try, somehow, to free the lion.

The last truck moved off, ascending stately through its gears. She turned up her jacket collar—it was still damp autumn here, not winter, as it was up north, and yet penetrating—and went down into the maze of concrete, trying to keep the white needle in sight.

She was nearing the end of the longest year of her life. It had been distended by loss, by suffering—by death, for it seemed to her that since she had seen she would die, in the mountains, and had accepted that, that she had in fact died; and when the ghostly sleds had appeared, creeping through the blowing snow with supernatural purpose and a faint wailing, it had taken her a time to understand that they had not come to signal the death she awaited but to thrust her back into life.

And then she had killed a man, an eternity later, when they had at last come down out of the mountains. A Federal man, one of the black coats, who still slogged through mud implacably toward her in dreams. That was a long moment, a year in itself. Yet it took her less time than it had taken Painter to kill the man who had come on them in the cabin in the woods, back at the beginning of her life.

Moving northwest with the widowed pride, always deeper into wilderness and solitude, always waiting for something, some word of Painter, some word from the fox, she felt her time expand vastly. Grief, waiting, solitude: if you want to live forever, she thought, choose those. In a way Caddie perceived but couldn't express, the pride did live forever, the females and the children: they lived within each moment forever, till the next moment. They took the same joy in the sunrise, hunted and played and ate with the same single-minded purpose, as they had when Painter had been with them; and their grief, when they felt it, was limitless, with no admixture of hope or expectation. She had explained to Meric: leos aren't like Painter, not most of them. Painter has been wounded into consciousness, his life is— a little bit—open to us, something shines through his being which is like what shines through ours, but the females and the children are dark. You'll never learn their story because they have no story. If you want to go among them, you have to give up your own story: be dark like they are.

Caddie by now knew how to do that, to an extent, but Meric would never learn it, and in any case it wasn't allowed to either of them then, because with Painter gone they two must act as the bridge between the pride and the human world it moved through and lived in. They had to spend Reynard's money in the towns, they had to learn the safe border crossings, they had constantly to *think*. Caddie forced herself to struggle against the wisdom of the females, fight it with human cunning for their sakes, forced herself to believe that only by keeping her head above the dark water could she help save them, when all she wanted to do was give up the burden of cunning and sink down amid their unknowing forever. No: only to Painter could she resign that burden.

Then at one of the prearranged mail drops had come the summons from the fox. Suspicious, anxious, unable to believe that Reynard could really know all he pretended to know, she had nevertheless left Meric to shepherd the pride and followed her instructions. It was all she could do.

She soon lost sight of the monument. The littered, shabby streets urged her on, striking purposefully through the buildings but leading nowhere except to further streets. Alarmed by acrid odors that had come to mean danger to her, she began to see why Painter had smoked tobacco in towns. She walked aimlessly among crowds that seemed bent on pressing business, hurrying people with eyes intent, lugging heavy bags that perhaps they were carrying somewhere or perhaps had stolen from somewhere they were eager to get away from. Caddie thrust her hands into her pockets and walked on, unable to catch anyone's eye or hold his attention long enough to ask a question.

At a convergence of streets, stores were lit up, and the sallow globes of a few unbroken streetlights were on. Lines of people stood patiently waiting to be let in one at a time to buy—what? Caddie wondered. In one barred store window, televisions: ranks of them, all showing the same image differently distorted, a man's head and shoulders, his mouth moving silently. Then, in an instant, they all changed, to show a street like this one. A black three-wheeled car. Two men in dark overcoats got out, looking wary and tired. Between them a third, a tiny limping creature, in a hat whose brim hid him from the camera, but whose manner revealed him to Caddie. She could almost smell him.

She went to the door of the store. A burly black guard, armed, stood in the doorway, looking bored. Caddie slipped past him, expecting to be seized, but the guard seemed not to care.

". . . has not revealed the identity of its witness, though he is believed to have been a high official in the Gregorius government. USE says facts revealed in the hearings will shed dramatic new light on the assassination of two years ago. . . ." He spoke with such a clipped, false intonation that she could barely understand him.

Someone stepped in front of her then; and another, coatless— he must work here, she thought—came to stand next to her. "This ain't a the-ayter," he said.

"What?"

The person in front of her stepped away. On the screen was an image that made her heart leap. Painter stood in front of his tent, his old shotgun in his hands. He looked at her—or at Meric, rather—calm, puzzled, faintly amused.

The store employee put his hand on Caddie's shoulder. "You ain't buyin'," he said. "Go home and watch it."

She pulled away from him, desperate to hear. The guard at the door glanced over, and proceeded toward her ponderously.

She heard the clipped, brisk voice say: "Government channels are silent." And Painter was replaced by a smiling woman standing next to a television, which showed the same woman and the same television, which showed her again.

✳

The monument she found at last stood at the end of an oblong pool, empty now and a receptacle for the litter of those camped on the sward of brown grass around it. For the height of a man the monument was marked with slogans, most of them so covered with other slogans as to be unreadable. It rose above these, though, to a chaste height. When Caddie looked up at it it seemed to be in the act of tumbling on her.

She went carefully around the perimeter of the park again and again, slowly, without much hope. Reynard between those men had obviously been a prisoner. How could he meet her here if he wasn't free? She studied the knots of people gathered around fires lit in corroded steel drums, looking for his small face, sure she wouldn't see it.

Night made it certain. She was trying to decide which of the fires she would approach, how she could buy food, when a bearded man, smiling, put a paper into her hand. WHERE IS HE NOW? the paper shouted, and beneath this was a grotesque picture of what might be a leo. Startled, she looked up. The man reminded her of Meric, despite the beard, despite the sunken chest and long neck: something gentle and self-effacing in his eyes and manner. She tried to read the paper, but could only pick out words in the last light: civil rights, nature, leo, crimes, USE, freedom, Sten Gregorius.

He must have seen the look of wonderment on her face, because he turned back to her after handing out more of the sheets. "Here," he said, digging into a pocket, "wear a button." He wore one like the one he gave her: the cartoon of the leo, and under it the words BORN FREE.

She didn't know how any of this had come about, but this man must be a friend. She wanted desperately to tell him, to ask him for help; but she didn't dare. She only looked at him, and at the button. He turned to go. She said: "Will you be here tomorrow?"

"Here or over there," he said, pointing to where a pillared

shrine was lit garishly by spotlights. "Every day. If I'm not in jail." He made a sudden, aggressive gesture with upraised fist, but his inoffensive face still smiled. She let him go, with a sinking heart.

She was not alone. There were others who knew about Painter. Many others. She didn't know if that was good or bad. She slipped in among a silent crowd around a fire at the base of the monument, the strange button clutched in her hand like a token, and rested her back against the stone. Her last meal had been hours ago, but she hardly noticed that she was hungry; hunger had come, over the months, to seem her natural state.

✳

"They'll bring him out in a moment," Barron said. "Yes. There. There he is."

The room they stood in was a consulting room of what had once been a public mental hospital meant for the dangerous insane. It was empty now, except for its single prisoner or patient; he had been installed here because no one could think of anywhere else to put him: no other cage.

The window of the consulting room looked out on the exercise yard, a high box of blackened brick, featureless. The single rusted steel door that led into the yard opened. Nothing could be seen within. Then the leo came out.

Even at this distance, and even though he was draped in an old army greatcoat, Reynard could see that he was thin and damaged. He walked aimlessly for a moment, taking small steps. He seemed constricted; then Reynard saw that his wrists were shackled. He wondered briefly if they had had to smith special shackles for those wrists. Painter went to the one corner of the blind court where thin sunlight fell in a long diagonal, and sat, lowering himself carefully to the ground. He rested his back against the blank brick and looked out at nothing, unmoving. Now and again he moved his arms within the shackles, perhaps because they chafed, perhaps because from moment to moment he forgot they were on him.

"What have you done to him?" Reynard asked.

"His condition is his own fault," Barron said quickly. "He

won't eat, he won't respond to therapy." He turned from the window. "As far as we can tell, he's physically unimpaired. Just weak. Of course he makes difficulties when we try to examine him."

"I think," Reynard said, "your prisoner is dying."

"Wrong. He has injections daily. Almost daily." As though trying to draw Reynard with him away from the window, he went to the far end of the room and perched on a dusty metal desk. "And he's not a prisoner. He's a subject of the USE Hybrid Species Project research arm. Technically, an experimental subject."

"Ah."

"Anyway, you've seen him. Now can we begin? You understand," he went on, "that I don't have any governmental authority. I can't make any legal deals."

"Of course."

"I can only act as a mediator."

"I think it'll do."

"This shouldn't enter into it," Barron said, looking at his knuckles, "but you, you personally, have made enormous difficulties for the government. Just enormous. It would be completely within their rights just to seize you and try you, or . . ."

"Or toss me down there. I know that. I think that what I have to offer will outweigh any vengeful feelings."

"Sten Gregorius."

"Yes. Where he is now, who his people are, the evidence against them, everything."

"We don't have much reason to believe you know all of that."

"My information regarding him"—he gestured toward the yard below the window—"was accurate enough."

"It put us to a lot of trouble. Unnecessary trouble."

"Well."

"You might be merely planning to confuse us, tell lies. . . ."

"I've voluntarily put myself in your hands this time," Reynard said. "I'm helpless. I know that if I mislead you now, the full weight of your authority will fall on me. I'm sure also that you have, well, experimental methods of extracting truths. The research arm."

"That's an odious slander."

"Is it?"

"We wouldn't let you renege, that's true enough," said Barron testily.

"It's all I meant."

"And what you want in exchange. It doesn't seem enough. Not for such a betrayal."

Reynard turned to the window again and looked out. "Perhaps you feel more deeply about betrayal than I do." Barron had to lean out over the desk now to catch his hoarse whisper. "The answer is that I'm at the end of my powers. I've eluded your government so far because of a large fortune I managed to assemble working for Gregorius. That's gone now. I'm old, not well. I've spent my life in motion, but I can't run anymore. Eventually I'd be cornered, taken—" He paused, staring down into the yard. "Rather than have that happen, I'd prefer to trade the last of what I have for peace. For time to die peacefully in." He turned to Barron. "Remember," he said. "I'm not a man. I am the only, the first and last of me there will ever be. You know I'm sterile. I have no loyalties. Only advantages."

Barron didn't speak for a moment; the affectless voice had seemed to paralyze him. Then he cleared his throat, opened his briefcase and looked inside, closed it. Himself again. "So," he said briskly, "in exchange for immunity, and a pension or the like—we'll negotiate details—you're willing to give evidence that Sten Gregorius and yourself planned the murder of Gregorius; that USE had nothing to do with it; that the murderers weren't USE agents; that Sten Gregorius is still conspiring against the Federal provisional government in the Northern Autonomy. Nashe?"

"Nashe, I hear, is dead."

"Then what you have to say about her can't hurt her."

"There's the other thing I require," Reynard said.

"Yes."

"The leo."

Barron straightened. "Yes, I think that's odd."

"Do you?"

"It's also probably impossible. He's committed several crimes; he's very dangerous."

Reynard made a noise that might have been a laugh. "Look at him," he said. "I think you've broken his spirit. At least."

"The criminal charges . . ."

"Come now," Reynard said almost sharply. "You've said yourself he's not a prisoner. An experimental subject only. Well. Put an end to the experiment."

"He's still dangerous. It would be like . . . like . . ." He seemed to search unused places for a forgotten image. "Like releasing Barabbas to the populace."

Reynard said nothing. Barron supposed he had spoken over the creature's head. "He's part of the conspiracy, in any case," he said.

"A very small part," Reynard said. "He never understood it. He was used, first to help me, then to distract your attention. He worked well enough."

"He and his kind have gotten completely bound up together in the public mind with Sten Gregorius. That may have been an accident. . . ."

"No accident. It was due to your stupidity in persecuting the leos so—so artlessly. Sten took up their cause. It was ready-made. By you." He limped toward the desk where Barron still sat, and Barron drew back as though he were being approached by something repugnant. "Maybe I can put this so that you can see the advantage to you. You're planning a reservation somewhere for the leos, a kind of quarantine."

"In the Southeastern Autonomy."

"Well then. Once Sten is in your hands, and the leo has gone voluntarily to this reservation, the union will evaporate."

"He would never go voluntarily," Barron said. "These beasts never do anything voluntarily except make trouble."

"Let me talk to him. I could persuade him. He listens to me. I've been his adviser, his friend." No irony. This was presented as an argument only. Barron marveled: no thin skin of pretense was drawn over this creature's amorality. It made him easy to deal with. Only—

"Why," he said, "do you insist on this? It can't be just to make things easier for us."

Reynard sat on the edge of a metal folding chair. Barron wondered if he was at a loss. It seemed unlikely. He moved his hands on the head of his stick. His long feet just touched the floor. "Do you go to zoos?" he said at last.

"When I was a kid. In my opinion, zoos . . ."

"You might have noticed," Reynard went on, "that according to a curious human logic, the cages are proportionate in size to the creatures they contain. Small cages for small animals—weasels, foxes—big ones for big animals. In old zoos, anyway."

"Well?"

"People go to zoos. They pity the lions, noble beasts, caged like that, with hardly room to move. In fact the lion is relatively comfortable. He's a lazy beast and exerts himself only when he must—if he doesn't have to, he rests. Other animals—foxes, notably—have a natural urge for movement. In the wild, they may cover miles in a night. They pace endlessly in their little cages. All night, when the zoo is closed, they pace—two body lengths this way, two that way. For hours. They probably go mad quite quickly. A madness no one notices.

"To put it baldly: I would do anything to avoid the cage. I hope you grasp that. He—down there—probably doesn't care. So long as he has a cage suited to his dignity."

"The reservation."

"It's the least I can do for him," Reynard said, again with no irony. "The very least."

Barron stood and went to the window. The leo still sat; his eyes appeared to be closed. Was he sleeping? Maybe the fox was right. Barron had felt, though he had ignored, a certain pity for the leos who would be committed to quarantine. Left over from guilt over the Indian reservations, perhaps. But the Indians were, after all, men. Maybe the USE plan, besides being the only practicable one, was the kindest too.

"All right," he said. "When do you want to talk to him? I make no promises. But I agree in principle."

"Now," Reynard said.

✳

Face upward into the weak sun, Painter watched brilliance expand and deliquesce on his eyelids. Entranced by hunger, he had entered into a fugue of sleep, memory, waking, rough dream.

Coalescing in sunlight, fat, strong; taste of blood from cut lips, a haze of fury, then some victory—ancientest childhood. Sun and darkness, warmth of light and then warmth of flesh in lightlessness, amid other bodies. Sleep. Consciousness spring by spring flaring like anger along flesh wakened roughly, nothing father Sun could do against the father before him, his battle only, only perceived in enormous flashings of feeling, the possibility of victory, the battle prolonged, unacknowledged, he shackled and . . . Shackled. He raised his arms and opened his eyes. Vision of nothing. Still shackled. Stains of ancient rains ran across the yard, meeting at the drain in the center, rays from a minute black sun, tears from a deadeye.

Wandering. Nothing to do, nothing he couldn't do, coursing the stream of his own blood, turning and spinning on its currents. But bounded: banks of men, channeling him. He pressing on their united faces, passing through, they coalescing again behind and in front, rebounding him. Towns and roads. Strength for sale: cold steel half-dollars and paper as fine as shed snakeskin. As though in disguise he wore them. Smells burned him, tobacco burned smells, half-dollars bought both, language crept in between his eyes and came out his mouth tasting of tobacco. At a touch, anger could flare; they pressed so tightly together, how could they bear themselves? Learning how to bind down strengths and knit them up, twigs bound too tightly to burn. Until he was packed and pregnant as bound dynamite, faceless as quarried walls: the stone walls he square-cut in quarries, faceted walls all of one stone, like the faces that looked at him, faceted, unyielding, nothing could move them except dynamite.

The walls around him now were black; those had been pale. Would he die here? Sun had withdrawn from him. He would die here when Sun withdrew altogether; day by day it had grown narrower, a few minutes' blessing only now, tenderly feeling the brick wall brick by brick as it ascended away from him. Winter, and he would die in prison.

In prison. That was where he had been cut in two, in the darkness. Feeling the manskin peel away in the darkness like a separate being. Solitary. No place else to put you. Steel doors closing like cryings-out. Rage at the darkness. Too dumb to know better. Half a man, they said. Like the blond boy who kissed his hands for it, wept before him: not a man. They didn't know he had a man concealed on his person. Carrying a concealed weapon, resisting arrest, solitary: and in the darkness feeling the man peel away, as though he were a skin, and the manskin in darkness acquired his own life.

How long? Day after dark day he descended stairs, kept descending further stairs into further darkness, illuminating it with unyielding will, following the manskin that led the way. Solitary. Not alone though. Because the manskin led him. Down to the bottom of the darkness, his being held up before him like a torch, the manskin always just ahead, hair streaming from his head like language from his mouth; stepless darkness where they went down in the halo of his light-bearing aliveness. In the end, the bottom, and he made the manskin turn. No retreat. You are me. In the terrible dry light of understanding looking into his face, drawing close to his face, reaching for him, he for him, coupling ravishing, beast with two backs but ever after that one face only. He did not die in prison.

The fox came to him in prison. He thought at first he had invented him too. Not a prison like this one: white, naked, without surfaces, only the cryings-out of steel doors shrieking closed together. Get you out of here. What did he want? Nothing. Out of there: away from darkness, through the shrieking doors, into Sun's face again. Why?

Accept it as your due, the fox had said. Only accept it. You deserve my service; only accept it.

"Painter," said the fox.

Take me as your servant, he had said. Only go by my direction for a while. For a long while, maybe. Take what you deserve; I'll point it out to you.

"Painter," said the fox.

If this were the fox before him now in the black prison, he would kill him. The fox had betrayed him, freed him from the white prison so that he could die in the black; had given him over to the men. Had killed his son. Would kill him. Sun alone knew why he wanted such deaths. And if this were the fox

"Painter."

before him now he would

"Your servant," said the fox.

"You."

"I've come to get you out. Again."

"You put me here." His long-unused voice was thick.

"An error. A piece of planning that went badly. My apologies. It's worked out for the best."

"My son is dead."

"I'm sorry."

Painter moved his arms against the shackles. Reynard, hardly taller than he, though he stood, bent over him, leaning on his stick. "How ill are you?"

"I could still kill you."

"Listen to me now. You must listen. There is a way out of this."

"Why? Why listen?"

"Because," Reynard said, "you have no one else."

✳

From the window of the consulting room, Barron looked down on them. Like a scene from some antique cartoon or fairy-tale, seeing them together. Hideous, in a way. Misdirected ingenuity. Frankenstein. He wondered at the fox, though; had he been right, about his own nature? It would be interesting to see what limits there were to his intelligence. Certainly he was cunning, cold, in a way no man could be; but still he apparently had been unable to see that the price he had asked for his betrayal was too high, and that to leave him in peace was something the government couldn't possibly do. Once Reynard was of no more use to them, he certainly couldn't be set free to do more mischief.

Tests, maybe. It would be interesting to see. A misdirected experiment, perhaps, and yet perhaps something could be learned from it.

What were they saying? He cursed himself for not having foreseen this, not having the courtyard bugged.

✻

In the morning, Caddie found a food shop and ate, pressed in among other bodies, watching the windows steam up and the steam condense to tears that streaked the panes. An argument started and threatened to become a fight. Everyone here seemed touchy, frustrated, at flashpoint. What did they want so badly, which they weren't getting? What was it that goaded them?

She began her circuit of the park again, carefully studying faces and places, wondering what she could do alone, if she couldn't find Reynard. Nothing. She had no idea where Painter was. *Government channels are silent.* But she couldn't give up, not after having come so far, counted so much on this plan, readied herself so carefully for any sacrifice. . . . She found that she was hurrying, not searching, driven by anxiety. She stopped, and closed her eyes. No hope, she must have no hope. When her heart was calm, she opened her eyes. At an intersection of streets not far off was a slim, black three-wheeler, closed and faceless.

She approached it by stages, uncertain, and not wanting to reveal herself. When she passed by it, walking aimlessly and not looking at it, as though passing by chance, the passenger door was pushed open by a stick. "Get in," Reynard whispered.

His traveling den smelled richly of him, though he himself was obscure in the shuttered darkness. The man up front was uniformed. Caddie looked from him to Reynard, uncertain.

"My jailer," Reynard said. His harsh sandpaper voice was fainter than ever. "On our side, though. More or less."

Still not knowing how freely she could speak, Caddie gave him the paper the bearded man had given her. She saw Reynard's spectacles glint as he bent over it, his nose almost touching it. He folded it, thoughtful.

"It's Meric Landseer who's done this," he said at last. "Yes. His tapes. Prepare ye the way of the Lord. Well. It'll do. Yes."

He put the paper back in her hand, and leaned close to her, seizing her wrist in the strong, childlike grip she had first felt in the woods, in the hollow tree. "Now listen to me and remember everything I say. I'm going to tell you where Painter is. I'm going to tell you what he must do to be free, and what the price is, and what you must do. Remember everything."

When he had told her, though, she refused. He said nothing, only waited for her answer. She felt she would weep. "I can't," she said.

"You must." He stirred, impatient or uncomfortable. "We don't have time here to talk. If I'm missed, they'll suspect something. They'll prevent this. Now I'll tell you: it was I who sent the Federals to the Preserve, to arrest Painter. Do you understand? Because of me he's where he is. He might have died. He will die, now, if he's not freed. His son. I murdered him. By what I did. Do you understand? All my fault. You might have starved. His wives and children. All my fault. Do you understand?"

He had taken her wrist again, and squeezed insistently. She looked at his black shape, feeling well up in her a disgust so deep that saliva gathered in her mouth, as though she would spit at him. Alien, horrid, as unfeeling as a spider. She wanted desperately to leave, to do this without him, but she knew she couldn't. "All right," she said thickly.

"You'll do it."

"Yes."

"Exactly as I said."

"Yes."

"Remember everything."

"Yes." She pulled her wrist from his fingers. He pushed open the door with his stick.

"Go," he said.

She went across the street to the park, pulling up her jacket collar against the cold wind, which blew papers and filth against her ankles as she walked. She wouldn't weep. She'd think of Painter and Painter's son only. As though she were an extension of the gun and not the reverse, she would execute its purposes. She wouldn't *think*.

The pillared shrine contained only an enormous seated figure Caddie thought she should know but couldn't remember. His name, most of his left leg, and some fingers had been erased by a bomb. The black rays of the blast still flashed up the pillars and across the walls as though frozen at the moment of ignition. The same desperate and illegible slogans marked this monument, sprayed across the slogans cut in stone. With malice toward none, and justice for all.

Vengeance.

At the side of the building the bearded man sat on the steps, eating hard-boiled eggs from a paper and talking animatedly to a group of men and women gathered around him. The step was littered with eggshell and his beard was flecked with yoke.

"Brutality," he was saying. "What does that mean? It doesn't matter what *they* do. Their morality isn't ours, it can't be. It's enough that *we* see the right in our terms, and if we see it we *must* act on it. The basis of all political action . . ."

He turned and looked at her, munching. She gave him back the paper he had given her, with the picture of the leo on it.

"I know where he is," she said.

*

"Without the shackles," Reynard said.

"We can't," Barron said. "How do we know what he'll do?"

"A crowd of people is outside," Reynard said. "They've been waiting all night. Do you want them to see him shackled?"

"Well, why did you delay us all night?" Barron's voice was a tense whisper attempting a shout. It was hideously cold in the corridors of the old hospital; he felt tremors of anxiety and cold and sleeplessness contract his chest. The corridors were dim; only every third or fourth light was lit, glaring off the parti-colored green enamel of the walls, as though the place were lit with fading flares. "We'll take him out a back way."

"I think they've discovered all the exits."

The guards and overcoated marshals whom Barron had brought in to organize this release stood around looking stupidly efficient, waiting for orders to execute. "We'll have to get the van around to the back."

"They'll follow that for sure. Leave the van where it is. Send some people out the front way, to make it look as though he were coming out that way. Then we'll go out the back. The car that brought me is across the street; one of your people is driving it. Use that."

"That's crazy," Barron said. He was in an agony of indecision. "How did all those people *find* this place? What do they want?"

"However they did," Reynard said, almost impatiently, "they certainly won't go away until the leo is gone. In fact, more are collecting." He looked at the marshals, who nodded. "You'll have a mass demonstration if you don't act quickly."

Barron looked from the marshals to the door through which the leo was to come. He had meant it all to be so simple. The leo would walk freely out of the building and into a waiting van. A single camera would record it. Tomorrow, his arrival at the barracks in Georgia. The news would show it, with understated commentary. Later, when a fully articulated program had been developed, the film would be a powerful incentive to other leos.

All spoiled now. The leo refused to leave unless Reynard was present. Reynard fussed and delayed. The crowd condensed out of the city like fog. And Barron was frightened. "All right," he said. "All right. We'll do that. We'll take him to that car. You'll remain here." He steeled himself. "I'll go with him."

Reynard said nothing for a moment. Then his pink tongue licked his dark lips: Barron could hear the sound it made. "Good," he said. "It's brave of you."

"Let's get it over with." He signaled to the marshals. From the car he could radio to be met somewhere. He wouldn't have to be alone with the leo for more than ten minutes. And the driver would be there. Armed.

They opened the heavy doors along the corridor, and signals were passed down. A dark figure appeared at the hallway's end, and came toward them. Two guards on each side, and two waiting at each branching corridor. He passed beneath the glare of the lights, in and out of pools of darkness. The men at his side, since they chose not to touch him as guards usually do, appeared more like attendants. The leo, draped in his overcoat, seemed to be making some barbaric kingly progress past the guards, beneath the lights.

He stopped when he reached Reynard.

"Take off the shackles," Reynard whispered. The attendants looked from the fox to Barron. Barron nodded. He must retain control of this situation; his must be the okay. He chose not to look at the leo; a glimpse showed him that the leo's face was passive, expressionless.

The shackles fell to the floor with a startling clatter.

"Down here," Barron said, and they began a procession—marshals, Barron, Reynard, the leo, more marshals, a hurried, undignified triumph: only the leo walked a measured pace.

Through the dirty glass of the back exit they could see the deserted street lit by a single dim streetlight and the pale light of predawn. Across the street, down another street, they could just make out where the three-wheeler was.

"Can't we get him closer?" Barron said. "You. Go over and tell him . . ." A knot of people appeared in the street, searching. Someone pointed to the door they stood behind; then the group turned away, running, apparently to summon help.

"Don't wait," Reynard said. "Do it now."

Barron looked up at the leo's huge, impassive face, trying to discover something in it. "Yes," he said; and then, loudly, as people do to someone they aren't sure will understand, he said: "Are you ready now?"

The leo nodded almost imperceptibly. Reynard, at his elbow—he came not much higher, stooped as he was now—said: "You know what to do." The leo nodded again, looking at nothing.

Barron took hold of the bar that opened the door. "You," he said, sectioning out with his hand some of the marshals, "watch here till we get off. The rest of you take him"—Reynard—"to the front, to the van. If they want something to look at, they can look at him. Quick."

With some bravado, he pushed open the door and held it for the leo, who went out and down the steps without waiting. From both ends of the street, people appeared, sudden masses, as though floodgates had been opened. Barron saw them; his head swiveling from side to side, he skipped to catch up with the leo. He reached up as though to take the beast's elbow, but thought better of it. The car was just ahead. The crowd hadn't yet seen them.

Good-bye, Barron, Reynard thought. Exhaustion swept him; he felt faint for a moment. The marshals collected around him and he raised a hand to make them wait a moment. He leaned on the stick. Only one more thing to do. He summoned strength, and straightened himself, leaning against the glass door facing the marshals. "All right," he said. "All right." Then he raised the stick, as though to indicate them.

The charge in the stick killed one marshal instantly, hurtling him into the others; two others it wounded. It threw Reynard, wrist broken, out the door and into the street. He began to scuttle rapidly across the pavement, his mouth grimacing with effort, his arms outstretched as though to break an inevitable fall. The crowd had swollen hugely in an instant; when it heard the blast and saw Reynard come stumbling out, it flowed around him as he went crabwise down the street opposite the way Barron and Painter had gone. Behind him, the marshals, guns drawn, came running; the crowd shrieked as one at the guns and the blood, and tried to stop their motion, but they were impelled forward by those behind.

The cameraman turned on his lights.

One person pushed out of the crowd toward the hurrying figure, ran toward him as the marshals ran after him, the marshals unable to fire because of the crowd. The swiveling, jostled blue light turned them all to ghastly sculptured friezes revealed by lightning.

Caddie reached the fox first. The crowd, impelled by her, surged close to the wounded, spidery creature. He grasped Caddie's arm.

"Now," he whispered. "Quick."

Quick, secret as a handshake, unperceived clearly by anyone —later the police would study the film, trying to guess which one of the fleeting, flaring, out-of-focus faces had been hers, which hand held the momentary glint of gun—she fired once, twice, again into the black creature who seemed about to embrace her. The gun sounds were puny, sudden, and unmistakable; the crowd groaned, screamed as though wounded itself, and struggled to move back, trampling those in back. Caddie was swallowed in it.

They made a wide circle around the fox. The blue light played over him; his blood, spattering rapidly on the pavement, was black. He tried to rise. The marshals, guns extended, shouting, surrounded him like baying hounds. His spectacles lay on the pavement; he reached for them, and stumbled. His mouth was open, a silent cry. He fell again.

Far off, coming closer, sirens wailed, keening.

EIGHT

Hieraconpolis; six views from a height

Very soon he would start south. His children had already departed, and he saw his wife less and less often as she scouted farther south. That evening she would not return; and soon winter would pinch him deeply enough to start him too toward the warmth. He lingered because he was ignorant; he had never made the journey, didn't know from repetition that the summons he felt was that summons. His first winter he had spent in the warmth of an old farmhouse; the second he had been flung into late, and he had only managed, mad with molt and cold and near-starvation, to come this far before spring saved him.

Returning at evening to the empty tower over the brown and suddenly unpopulated marshes, he had seen the big blond one arrive on foot; watched him tentatively explore the place. Then he slept. Men were of little interest to Hawk, though they didn't frighten him; he had lived much in their company. The following day another arrived, smaller, dark. The first visitor pointed Hawk out to the second where he stood on the tower top. Hawk went off hunting, deeply restless, and caught nothing all day. He stood sleepless long into the night, feeling the pressure of the wheeling stars on his alertness.

Below him in the shed, Caddie pressed herself against Painter, squirmed against him as though trying to work herself within the solidity of his flesh; tears of relief and purgation burned her eyes and made her tremble. She stopped her ears, too full of horrors, with the deep, continual burr of his breath, pressed her wet face against the drum of his chest. She wanted to hear, smell, touch, know nothing else now forever.

The next morning she was awakened by the growing burr of an engine. Painter was awake and poised beside her. She thought for a moment that she was in Reynard's cabin in the woods, where in her dream she had been sleeping. The engine came close—a small motor-bike, no, two. Painter with silent grace rose, stepped to the boarded window, and peered through the slats.

"Two," he said. "A blond boy. A dark girl."

"Sten," Caddie said. "Sten and Mika!"

She rose, laughing with relief. Painter, uncertain, looked from her to the door when it opened. Morning light silhouetted the bearded youth for a moment.

"Sten," Caddie said. "It's all right."

Sten entered cautiously, watching Painter, who watched him. "Where's Reynard?" he said quietly.

Painter said: "Shut the door."

Mika slipped in behind Sten, and Sten shut the door. The leo sat, slowly, without wasted motion, reminding Sten of an Arab chief taking a royal seat on the rug of his tent. The room was dim, tigered by bars of winter sunlight coming in through holes in the boarded windows, spaces in the old walls.

"You're Painter," Sten said. The leo's eyes seemed to gather in all the light there was in the room, to glow in his big head like gems cut cabochon. They were incurious.

"All right," he said.

"We thought you were dead," Mika said.

"I was." He said it simply.

"Why did you come here?" Sten said. "Did Reynard . . . How did you get away from them?" He looked from the leo to the girl, who looked away. "Where is Reynard? Why are you here and not him?"

"Reynard is dead," Caddie whispered, not looking up.

"Dead? How do you know?"

"She knows," Painter said, "because she killed him."

Caddie's face was in her hands. Sten said nothing, unable to think of the question that would make sense of this.

Eyes still covered, unwilling to look at them, Caddie told them what had happened; she told them about the capital, about the hospital, the bearded man, tonelessly, as though it had happened to someone else. "He made me," she said at last, looking up at them. "He made me do it. He said there was no other way of getting Painter free except to trade him for you, Sten. And there was no way he could keep from telling all he knew about you unless he was dead. So we planned it. We made a distraction at the hospital—the crowd—so Painter could get away. He said it was the only way." She pleaded with them silently. "He said he longed for it. He said, 'Do it right; do it well.' Oh, Jesus . . .'"

Mika came to her and sat beside her, put her arm around her, moved to pity. Horrible. She thought Caddie would weep, but she didn't; her eyes were big, dark, and liquid as an animal's, but dry. She took Mika's hand, accepted absently her comfort, but was uncomforted.

No one spoke. Her brother sat down warily opposite Painter. Mika felt, in spite of the golden, steady regard in the leo's eyes, that he saw nothing, or saw something not present, as though he were a great still ghost. What on earth was to become of them? They lived at the direction of beasts. Reynard had used Caddie as he might a gun he put into his mouth. In the mountains with the leos she had witnessed inexplicable things. Now in the shuttered shack she felt intensely the alien horror that Reynard had inspired in her the first time she had seen him; the same horror and wrongness she felt when she thought of certain sexual acts, or terrible cruelties, or death.

"He sent us both here," Sten said softly to the leo. "He must have meant for us to meet." He raised his head, tightened his jaw in a gesture Mika knew meant he was uncertain, and wanted it not to show. "It's my plan, when things are—further along, to protect you. All of you. To offer you my protection."

Mika bit her lip. It was the wrong thing to say. The leo didn't stir, but the charge that ran between him and her brother increased palpably. "Protect yourself," he said. Then nothing more.

They were engaged in some huge combat here, Mika felt, but whether against the leo or beside him, and for what result, she didn't know. And the only creature who could resolve it for them was dead.

✳

There are bright senses and dark senses. The bright senses, sight and hearing, make a world patent and ordered, a world of reason, fragile but lucid. The dark senses, smell and taste and touch, create a world of felt wisdom, without a plot, unarticulated but certain.

In the hawk, the bright senses predominated. His scalpel vision, wide and exact and brilliantly hued, gave him the world as a plan, a geography, at once and entire, without secrets, a world that night (or—in his youth—the hood) annihilated utterly and day re-created in its entirety.

The dog made little distinction between day and night. His vision, short-sighted and blind to color, created not so much a world as a confusion, which must be discounted; it only alerted him to things that his nose must discover the truth about.

The hawk, hovering effortlessly—the merest wing shift kept him stable above the smooth-pouring, endlessly varied earth—perceived the dog, but was not himself perceived. The dog held little interest for him, except insofar as anything that moved beneath him had interest. He recorded the dog and its lineaments. He included the dog. He paid him no attention. He knew what he sought: blackbird on a reed there, epaulet of red. He banked minutely, falling behind the blackbird's half circle of sight, considering how best to fall on him.

Through a universe of odors mingled yet precise, odors of distinct size and shape, yet not discrete, not discontinuous, always evolving, growing old, dying, fresh again, the dog Sweets searched for one odor always. It needed to be only one part in millions for him to perceive it; a single molecule of it among ambient others could alert his nose. Molecule by molecule he had spun, with limitless patience and utter attention, the beginnings of a thread.

The thread had grown tenuous, nearly nonexistent at times; there were times he thought he had lost it altogether. When that happened, he would move on, or back, restless and at a loss until he found it again. His pack, not knowing what he sought or why, but living at his convenience—usually without argument—followed him when he followed the thread of that odor. Somewhere, miles perhaps, behind him, they followed; he had left a clear trail; but he had hurried ahead, searching madly, because at last, after a year, the thread had begun to thicken and grow strong, was a cord, was a rope tugging at him.

Some days later. Flying home from the margins of the gray sea, weary, talons empty. From a great height he saw the man moving with difficulty over the marshy ground: followed his movements with annoyance. Men caused the world to be still, seek cover, lie motionless, swamp-colored and unhuntable, for a wide circle around themselves: some power they had. The man looked up at him, shading his eyes.

Loren stopped to watch the hawk fall away diagonally through the air as cleanly and swiftly as a thrown knife. When he could see him no longer, he went on, his boots caught in the cold, sucking mud. He felt refreshed, almost elated. That had been a peregrine: it had to be one of his. At least one bird of his had lived. It seemed like a sign. He doubted he would ever read its meaning, but it was a sign.

The tower seemed deserted. There was no activity, no sign of habitation. It seemed somehow pregnant, waiting, watching him; but it always had, this was its customary expression. Then his heart swelled painfully. A tall, bearded boy came from the tower door, and saw him. He stopped, watching him, but didn't signal. Loren, summoning every ounce of calm strength he owned, made his legs work.

As he walked toward Sten, an odd thing happened. The boy he had carried so far, the Sten who had inhabited his solitude, the blond child whose eyes were full of promise sometimes, trust sometimes, contempt and bitter reproof most times, departed from him. The shy eyes that met his now when he came into the tower yard didn't reflect him; they looked out from Sten's real true otherness and actuality, and annihilated in a long instant the other Sten, the Sten whom Loren had invented. With relief and trepidation, he saw that the boy before him was a stranger. Loren wouldn't embrace him, or forgive him, or be forgiven by him. All that had been a dream, congress with phantoms. He would have to offer his hand, simply. He would have to smile. He would have to begin by saying *hello*.

"Hello," he said. "Hello, Sten."

"Hello, Loren. I hoped you'd come."

So they talked there in the tower yard. Someone seeing them there, looking down from a height, would not have heard what they said, and what they said wasn't important, only that they spoke, began the human call-and-response, the common stichomythy of strangers meeting, beginning to learn each other. In fact they talked about the hawk that floated far up, a black mark against the clouds.

"Could it be one you brought in, Loren?"

"I think it must be."

"We can watch it and see."

"I doubt if I could tell. They weren't banded."

"Could it be Hawk?"

"Hawk? I don't think so. No. That would be . . . That wouldn't be likely. Would it."

A silence fell. They would fall often, for a while. Loren looked away from the blond boy, whose new face had already begun to grow poignantly familiar to him, terribly real. He ran his hand through his black hair, cleared his throat, smiled; he scuffed the dead grass beneath his feet. His heart, so long and painfully engorged, so long out of his body, began to return to him, scarred but whole.

❋

Painter lay full length on his pallet at the dark end of the building Loren had once lived in. The cell heater near him lit his strange shape vaguely. He lifted his heavy head when they came in, easeful, careful. If he had been observing them in the tower yard he gave no sign of it.

"A friend," Sten said. "His name is Loren Casaubon. My best friend. He's come to help."

The leo gazed at him a long time without speaking, and Loren allowed himself to be studied. He had often stood so, patiently, while some creature studied him, tried to make him out; it neither embarrassed nor provoked him. He stared back, beginning to learn the leo, fascinated by what he could see of his anatomy, inhaling his odor even as the leo inhaled his. Half-man, half-lion, the magazines and television always said. But Loren knew better, knew there are no such things as half-beasts: Painter was not half-anything, but wholly leo, as complete as a rose or a deer. An amazing thing for life to have thrown up: using man's ceaseless curiosity and ingenuity, life had squared its own evolution. He almost laughed. Certainly he smiled: a grin of amazement and pure pleasure. The leo was, however he had come about, a beautiful animal.

Painter rose up. His prison weakness had not quite left him; now, when he stood, a sudden blackness obtruded between him and the man who stood before him. For a brief moment he knew nothing; then found himself supported by Sten and Loren.

"Why did you come here?" he said.

"Reynard sent me. To help Sten."

The leo released himself from them. "Can you hunt?"

"Yes."

"Can you use those?" He pointed to Loren's old rabbit wires hung in a corner.

"I made them," Loren said.

"We'll live, then," Painter said. He went to where the snares were hung and lifted them in his thick graceless fingers. Traps. Men were good at those. "Can you teach me?" he asked.

"Teach you to be a trapper?" Loren smiled. "I think so."

"Good." He looked at the two humans, who suddenly seemed far away, as though he looked down on them from a height.

Since the moment in the dead city when he had seen that there was no escape from men, no place where their minds and plans and fingers couldn't reach, a flame had seemed to start within him, a flame that was like a purpose, or a goal, but that seemed to exist within him independently of himself. It was in him but not of him. It had nearly guttered in the black prison, but it had flamed up brightly again when he had taken the man Barron in his grip. In the days he had lain with Caddie on the pallet here in the darkness he had begun to discern its shape. It was larger than he was; he was a portal for it only. Now when he looked at the men and saw them grow small and far-off, it flared up hotly, so hotly that it blew open the doors of his mouth, and he said to them, not quite knowing why or what he meant: "Make me a trapper. I will make you hunters of men."

✳

Furious, Hawk broke his stoop and with a shriek of bitter rage flung himself toward the prongs of a dead tree. The rabbit struggling on the ground, hurt, helpless, had been the first edible creature he had seen all day. And just as he was diving to it with immense certainty, already tasting it, the big blond one had stamped out of the weeds with a shout.

Hawk observed the intruder mantle over the rabbit. He roused, and his beak opened with frustrated desire. They were driving him off: from his home, from his livelihood. The wind, too, pressed him to go, creeping within his plated feathers and causing the ancient tree to creak. Unknown to him, a family of squirrels lay curled inside the tree, not far below where he sat, utterly still, nosing him, alert with fear. Hawk didn't see the squirrels: there were no squirrels there.

Painter slit the twitching rabbit's throat neatly and then attempted to take it from the snare. He knew he must think, not pull. There was a plan to this. His unclever fingers moved with slow patience along the wire. He could learn this. He suggested that the man within him take a part: help him here.

He gutted the rabbit, and slit its ankle at the tendon; then he slipped one foot through the slit he had made so that the rabbit could be carried. The hitch was neat, satisfying, clever. He wouldn't have thought of it: the boy Sten had shown it to him.

The long prison weakness was sloughing away from him; and even as his old strengths were knitting up in him, cables tempered somehow by loss, by imprisonment, he felt his being knitted together too, knitted into a new shape. Carrying the rabbit, enjoying the small triumph of the snare, he went up a low hill that gave him a view over the wide marshland. The feeble sunlight warmed him. He thought of his wives, far off somewhere; he thought of his dead son. He didn't think anything about them; he came to no conclusions. He only thought of them. The thoughts filled him up as a vessel, and passed from him. He was emptied. Wind blew through him. Wind rushed through him, bright wind. Something brilliant, cold, utterly new filled him as with clear water. He knew, with a certainty as sudden as a wave, that he stood at the center of the universe. Somehow—by chance even, perhaps, probably, it didn't matter—he had come to stand there, be there, be himself that center. He looked far over the winter-brown world, but farsighted as he was he couldn't make out the shape of what lay at his frontiers, and didn't attempt to. From all directions it would come to him. He thought: if I were raised up to a high place, I would draw all men to me.

His wide gaze turned the world. He saw, far off, the dog, coming toward him, squirming through the reeds and mud. Even as he looked, the dog barked, calling to him.

Sweets didn't need to call again, he already lived within Painter; the dark shape far off on the hill was only the rich, imperious center of him, he extended infinitely out from it; Sweets had been drawn to him by only the faintest, the most tenuous, the farthest-extended atoms of his being. It had been enough. Now Sweets needed only to plunge into that center, taste it with his tongue, to forget that anything else existed.

Painter waited on the hill, watching the dog hunching and leaping and struggling toward him.

✳

Winter deepened toward the death of the sun. On the eve of the solstice, Hawk could refuse the insistent summons no more. He had come back to his evening rest, but perceived as he approached it that there was someone there in the tower. He circled it for a time. He didn't, anyway, want to rest; he wanted to fly, soar, beat away night with long wings. This world had grown old. He rose up in easy stages, seeking a quick current.

As he went, Loren and Sten watched him, passing back and forth Loren's binoculars.

"The glint," Sten said. "When the light catches it . . . See?"

"Yes."

"His jesses. The grommets in them."

"It must be."

"It *was* Hawk."

"I think it was. I don't know how."

"Next year, will he come back?"

"Maybe."

"We could take him, take him up."

"No." Loren had read the sign. "Not after he's been free. There's no caging him now. He's nobody's hawk now, Sten." He didn't say: and neither are you.

He shifted the binoculars. Far off, something hovered: not a bird. It seemed to dart, searching, like a preying dragonfly. Then, moving straight toward them, swiftly: they could hear it.

All of them in the tower heard it. Below, Mika looked out the slats of the windows; Sweets lifted his ears and growled deep in his throat, till Painter stilled him.

"It's coming here," Mika said. "It's black."

Like a hawk, it hung for a time thoughtfully overhead, moving only slightly, looking (they all felt it) down on prey it knew was there, however concealed. Then it dropped; its noise grew loud and its vortex hurtled away dead leaves and chaff, dust of weeds and winter detritus. Its blades slowed, but continued to slice air. Its bubble face was tinted, they couldn't see anything within. Then it opened.

The pilot leapt out. Without looking around him he began to haul out boxes, crates, stores. He threw them out anyhow; one box of shiny aluminum containers broke open and spilled its contents like treasure. He pulled out three long guns and added them to the pile. He put his head within the interior. He stood aside while his passenger, with some difficulty, got out; then he clambered quickly back in and closed the bubble. The blades roared; their visitor bent over, closing his eyes against the machine's rising, his cape snapping around him. Then he straightened, tidying himself.

Reynard stood in the tower courtyard, leaning on a stick, waiting.

They came slowly from their hiding places. Reynard nodded to them as they came forth, pointing to each one with his stick. "Mika," he said. "And Caddie. Sten, and, and Loren. Where is the leo, Painter?"

"You're dead," Caddie said, staying far from him. "I killed you."

"No," he said. "Not dead." He walked toward her, not limping now, and she retreated; he seemed brisk, young, almost gay.

"I shot you." She giggled, a mad, strangled laugh.

"The one you shot," Reynard said, "was my parent. I am his —child. In a sense. In another sense, I am he almost as much as he was." He looked around at them. "It would be convenient for you to regard me as him." He grinned, showing the points of yellow teeth. "How anyway could Reynard the Fox die?"

Painter had come out of the shed, and Sweets, who curled his lip at the fox's odor. Painter came across the yard to where the little figure awaited him.

"Good evening, Counselor," he said.

"Hello, Painter."

"You're supposed to have died."

"Well, so I did. It's wrong, I know, for Judas to be the one to rise from the grave. But there it is." He looked a long time up at the massive face he had so often heard described and seen in tapes, but had never confronted. Even in the first moments of encounter he saw his parent's mistake, and wondered at it. "You shouldn't feel cheated," he said. "The one who betrayed you suffered death. But he wanted you to have his services still. My services. Forever.

"You see," he said, including them all, but looking at Painter intently, and at Sten, "I am sterile. Sexless, in fact. Therefore, in order to go on, I must be re-created—cloned—from a cell of my own. My parent understood the impasse he had come to, and saw that the only way out of it was his own death. I had been prepared to succeed him. My education was to have been longer, but I was released when he died." He looked up at the wide sky. "It was a long wait."

Loren said: "He did that in secret? Matured a clone? And nobody knew?"

"He was—I am—rich enough. There are men I pay well. Skilled. All that. I am immortal, if I'm careful." He smiled again. "A less delightful prospect than you might imagine."

Sten said: "You know what he knows."

"I am he."

"You know his plans, then. Why we're here."

"He had no plan." Reynard's voice had grown thin and almost inaudible. Small plumes of frost came from his nostrils. Evening —the longest of the year—had gathered by degrees around them.

"No plan?"

"No." Slowly, as though crumpling, he sat. A tiny folded figure. "Men plan," he said. "I'm not a man. The appearance is a deception. All lies. Talk." He said the word like a tiny bark. "Talk."

Mika shivered violently. When she spoke, she felt her throat constricted. "You said Sten was to be a king."

"Yes? Well, so he is, I suppose."

Sten said: "What am I supposed to do?"

"That's up to you, isn't it? If you are a king."

Caddie said: "You said Painter was King of Beasts."

"I did. How was I to know it was the truth? My parent died learning it."

They had come close, to hear his delicate, rasping, exhausted voice. "I make no plans," he said. "I discern what is, and act accordingly. You can never trust me. I must act; it's my nature. I'll never stop. You. You make the future. You know yourselves. I will act in the world you make. It's all up to you." One by one, they sat or squatted around him, all but Painter, who still stood, remote, unmoving as an idol with eyes of jewel. It was still not yet night, though it had been twilight most of the day. They could still see one another's faces, strange, matte, like the faces of people asleep. Tomorrow, the day would be imperceptibly longer. The sun would stir in his long sleep.

"Whatever we are to do," Reynard said, "we are at least all

here. Everyone I know of. All but Meric. Well. He prepares the
way. Some way." He offered, with a tiny, long-wristed hand, a
place in the circle to Painter. He waited while the leo sat. The
dog crept in beside him.

"Small we begin?" Reynard said.